Dangerous Pranks

"Have you seen anyone sneaking around this place in the past couple of days?" I asked. "Especially anyone connected with GTT?"

"Oh, I'm sure those boys would never pull such a serious and dangerous prank." Montgomery shook his head firmly, then hesitated. "Well, *most* of them, in any case . . ."

He looked troubled. I was about to ask him what he meant by "*most* of them."

But before I could, I heard a piercing, terrified scream from somewhere outside that open window.

THE HARDY BOYS

Undercover Brothers®

Available from Simon & Schuster

HARDY
BOYS

Undercover Brothers™

FRANKLIN W. DIXON

#33 Killer Connections

BOOK THREE IN THE KILLER MYSTERY TRILOGY

Aladdin
New York   London   Toronto   Sydney

ALADDIN
An imprint of Simon & Schuster Children's Publishing Division
1230 Avenue of the Americas, New York, NY 10020
First Aladdin paperback edition March 2010
Copyright © 2010 by Simon & Schuster, Inc.
All rights reserved, including the right of reproduction
in whole or in part in any form.
ALADDIN is a trademark of Simon & Schuster, Inc., and related logo
is a registered trademark of Simon & Schuster, Inc.
THE HARDY BOYS MYSTERY STORIES is a trademark
of Simon & Schuster, Inc.
HARDY BOYS UNDERCOVER BROTHERS and related logo are
registered trademarks of Simon & Schuster, Inc.
For information about special discounts for bulk purchases, please
contact Simon & Schuster Special Sales at 1-866-506-1949 or
business@simonandschuster.com.
The Simon & Schuster Speakers Bureau can bring authors
to your live event. For more information or to book an event contact
the Simon & Schuster Speakers Bureau at 1-866-248-3049
or visit our website at www.simonspeakers.com.
Designed by Sammy Yuen Jr.
The text of this book was set in Aldine 401 BT.
Manufactured in the United States of America / 0110 OFF
10 9 8 7 6 5 4 3 2 1
Library of Congress Control Number 2009934091
ISBN 978-1-4169-8696-6
ISBN 978-1-4169-9900-3 (eBook)

TABLE OF CONTENTS

More Bad Blood

"No!" I cried. My breath came in ragged gasps as I ran. My legs ached. My heart was pounding out of my chest.

I shot a glance back. My pursuer was catching up. Another step and he'd be on me. His face was twisted in a determined grimace.

But I was determined too. I had to shake him. I dodged one way, then another.

Unfortunately, that wasn't enough to lose him.

"Gaaaarh!" the guy growled as he leaped forward.

"Oof!" I hit the ground hard. The guy landed on top of me, pinning me to the ground.

"Fourth down!" someone yelled from nearby. "Our ball, dude."

I groaned as I sat up. "Yo, Van," I complained to the guy who'd brought me down. "This isn't the NFL, you know."

"Sorry, Frank." Van flashed me a goofy grin. He was a big guy. Nice, but a little quick-tempered. He tended to get caught up in things. Even if one of those things was just a friendly game of football on the Green.

"No biggie. I think all my bones are still intact." I climbed to my feet and traded a fist bump with him. Then I tossed the ball to another player.

"Come on, Frank," Spencer Thane called as I brushed the dirt and snow off my clothes. "Huddle up."

Was Spencer giving me a funny look? I wasn't sure. But it wouldn't be too surprising. He was one of the few people at the Willis Firth Academy who knew who I really was.

See, I'm not really the exclusive New England prep school type. My brother Joe and I attend public school back home in Bayport. But for the past couple of weeks we'd been faking it at Firth. I was posing as a student. Joe was acting as handler for the school's mascot, a German shepherd dog named Killer.

That's because Joe and I are ATAC agents. ATAC stands for American Teens Against Crime. Our father, Fenton Hardy, started the group. It trains teens to work undercover missions where adult agents would stick out like a cat at a dog show. Joe and I had solved tons of tough cases so far.

But this was proving to be one of the toughest yet. Firth's headmaster, Dr. Darity, had called ATAC after a rash of trouble on campus. There had been some graffiti, some threats, an injured swim coach, and various other things.

A lot of the trouble seemed to revolve around a certain fraternity, Gamma Theta Theta—better known as GTT. Joe and I had figured out that one of GTT's pledges, a sophomore named Ellery Marks, was behind most of the problems. Ellery was rebelling against his father. He didn't want to follow the old man into the frat—or into the Brothers of Erebus, a secret society within GTT. He'd been so determined to prove his point that he'd accidentally killed one of his fellow pledges and nearly disfigured another. Thanks to his family's wealth and connections, though, the whole thing had been hushed up and most of the school still didn't know why Ellery had left campus so abruptly.

But it hadn't ended there. Before Joe and I could pack up and head home, we'd found a couple of buckets of blood that Ellery didn't know anything about. It seemed he wasn't the only one causing trouble at Firth.

Soon it became clear that Dr. Darity's daughter, Destiny, was the second troublemaker's target. Destiny was the only female student at Firth. She'd been kicked out of her old boarding school, and her father had convinced the trustees to let his daughter finish out her senior year at Firth.

Destiny had quickly proved herself as a star player on the soccer team. She'd also proved herself to be spoiled, reckless, and maybe a little psycho. That didn't make her too popular with most people. The one exception was a junior named Lee Jenkins. In the course of our investigation, Joe and I had discovered that Destiny and Lee were a secret couple. That was kind of a bummer for Joe. He'd thought Destiny had the hots for him, mostly because she kept breaking into his cottage and flirting with him. See? Kind of nuts.

Anyway, it turned out that Casey, a student from Destiny's old school, had a serious grudge against her. He'd transferred to Firth just to mess with her. Joe and I finally nabbed him right before a big soccer game between the two schools.

That had been yesterday. Firth had won the game, and the team had celebrated by crowning Destiny and Lee as co-MVPs. But when the two of them had sipped some PowerUp punch from the Winner's Cup trophy, they'd both started staggering around. The punch had been spiked with some sort of fast-acting drug. The two of them had ended up sleeping it off in the infirmary, while Joe and I sent a sample of the tainted PowerUp to ATAC for analysis. They'd promised us results sometime today.

While we waited, we were both still doing our best to keep blending in at Firth. In my case, that meant a casual game of football on the Green. Not bad work if you can get it.

I jogged over to join the huddle. It was a cool, crisp Sunday just after brunch. Students were playing games, wandering down the brick-paved walks, or just chilling on the Green.

My eyes wandered toward the imposing four-story facade of Firth Hall, the largest and oldest building on campus. I was just in time to see Dr. Montgomery hobbling down the steep stone steps with the help of his cane. Dr. Montgomery was the former headmaster of Firth. He'd retired a few years back but still lived on campus and knew just about everything that went on there. For instance, he'd found out about Joe and me, though we still weren't sure how. Probably not a big deal, considering the guy was about a million years old and couldn't even walk without that cane. But he and Spencer weren't the only ones who knew our true IDs.

Thinking about that made me glance at Spencer. He'd been there when we'd taken down Ellery, so that's how he knew. Ellery and his father knew too, of course, though they were both long gone by now. But what if they'd told anyone else? The thought made me uneasy.

ATAC HQ had been concerned too. They'd even considered pulling us out. But Joe and I had convinced them to let us stay a little longer to try to wrap up the mission.

Joe always says I worry too much. Maybe he's right. I did my best to shake it off and focus on the game. Spencer had taken charge of the huddle. No surprise there. The guy was a natural-born leader. He was a senior and the president of GTT.

Then I spotted something else that made my stomach twist. Only not from worry this time. It was Patton Gage. Patton was a junior who had been a suspect for a while, mostly because he was totally obsessed with getting into GTT. He'd been rejected the previous year, and things weren't looking too good for him this year, either.

Actually, *he* wasn't looking too good right now. His face was still red and blistered from the acid he'd been burned by during a hazing ritual. One of Ellery's nasty little pranks.

Patton didn't notice me watching him. He rushed toward another group of students farther down the Green. They were playing soccer, but Patton didn't seem dressed to join in. He was wearing a wool overcoat with nice slacks and dress shoes showing below them. It seemed a little formal for a lazy Sunday. But Patton was kind of an odd duck, so I didn't worry about it.

I saw him join the soccer group and start talking and waving his hands around, looking excited. That wasn't much to worry about either. Patton was a huge gossip. Still, I couldn't help wondering what new rumor he was spreading to try to fit in.

"Let's go!" Spencer exclaimed, breaking into my thoughts.

The others let out a cheer. I joined in, even though I had no idea what the next play was. Oh, well. Being in ATAC means being good at improvising.

The game started up again. But the QB had barely snapped the ball when loud, angry shouts rang out from the direction of the soccer game.

I glanced that way. My eyes widened when I saw one kid give another a hard shove. Several others were squaring off, yelling and looking upset. It didn't take special ATAC training to recognize an argument that was about to turn violent.

Spencer saw it too. "Whoa," he said. "What's going on over there?"

He dropped the football and hurried over. I was right on his heels, along with most of the others.

When we got there, the shouting was louder than ever. The soccer players were so caught up in their argument that it took a moment to get their attention. But finally Spencer broke through. Natural leader, remember?

"What's up, you guys?" he demanded.

One of the soccer players was a senior member of GTT. He answered first. "These jerks are ragging on Lee," he spat out, glaring at some of the others.

"What do you mean?" I asked, instantly on alert. Lee had never been a serious suspect in the mission. But he *had* been a victim. His grades had been messed with in the school's online system. Neither of our culprits had fessed up to that one. Then there was the Winner's Cup incident, of course. . . .

"We just found out who poisoned the Winner's Cup," a hawk-nosed blond kid said. "It was Lee!"

"What?" Spencer exclaimed. "That's crazy. Lee got sick from drinking that stuff, remember?"

"That's what's so sneaky about it." Hawknose narrowed his eyes. "He wanted GTT to feel sorry for him so they'd let him in."

"Are you nuts?" Another GTTer shook his head. "Lee was a shoo-in anyway."

"Yeah. Plus, he'd never do anything like that," Van put in.

"How can you say that?" Another kid frowned. "Lee's not really one of us. You never know what someone like that will do."

"Someone like that?" the first GTTer challenged him, fists at the ready. "What do you mean?"

"What do you *think* I mean? I always thought it was a stupid idea to let in a bunch of grubby scholarship kids."

I winced. Lee was one of the few Firth students who wasn't filthy rich. He was a working-class kid from Boston. Dr. Darity had arranged a scholarship fund for a few deserving kids who couldn't afford prep school tuition. So far Lee was the star of the program. Straight-A student. Top athlete. GTT pledge. And as Joe and I had witnessed, he was the newest member of the Brothers of Erebus, too. Whatever *that* meant.

The argument was deteriorating again. There were taunts, insults, cheap shots, and a few shoves. I shot an irritated look at Patton. He'd started all this; I wondered if he was enjoying it.

But Patton didn't even seem to be paying attention anymore. He was checking his watch.

"Look, guys," Spencer was saying loudly, doing his best to step between a couple of guys who looked ready to kill each other. "Let's just calm down and—"

"What's going on here, lads?" asked a loud voice with a heavy British accent.

I spun around. A man was standing there holding a microphone in one hand and a camcorder in the other. His blocky, ruddy face wore a smarmy smile. The rest of him wore a shiny tan suit. His collar was open halfway to his belly, revealing a carpet of chest hair.

"Now, I heard things were getting fraught and freaky here at fancy Firth," the newcomer said, flipping his gelled blond hair out of his face with a practiced move. "But I had no idea it was this frenzied!"

Toxic Twists and Turns

"Come on, boy. Please?" I stared at Killer. He stared back from halfway across the room. I lunged forward. He darted away, staying just out of reach.

"I always thought I loved dogs," I said through gritted teeth. "I'm starting to rethink that."

Clearly the feeling was mutual. Killer stopped and sat down. Still out of reach.

I sighed, trying not to let my annoyance show. That would just be letting him win.

"This is all your fault, you know," I informed him as I edged closer. "If you hadn't rolled in something gross during your morning walk, I wouldn't have needed to take off your collar to wash it. Which, by the way? *So* not what I signed on for. I mean, it's bad enough that Aunt Trudy makes me help with my own laundry back home. Now I'm doing laundry for a *dog*?"

Killer didn't show much sympathy. In fact, if I hadn't known better, I might have thought he was laughing at me. Man's best friend? No way. At least not when it came to me. He loved just about everybody else. His former trainer, Hunt Hunter. The majority of the Firth students and faculty. Perfect strangers. And most of all . . .

"Anybody home?"

It was Frank. Killer changed instantly. He leaped to his feet, racing over with happily wagging tail and lolling tongue.

Typical. Killer might be a tough, super-disciplined former police dog most of the time. But he was putty in Frank's hands.

"Don't let him out the door," I warned Frank. "His collar's off, and he's been enjoying his freedom a little too much. If you know what I mean."

Frank grinned. "You giving Joe a hard time, buddy?" He rubbed the dog on his furry ruff while Killer practically drooled with delight. "Come on, playtime's over, okay? Now sit."

Killer instantly dropped to his haunches. Frank grabbed the collar out of my hand and snapped it on.

"Good boy," he told the dog. Then he shot me a sly look. "So what's the big deal?"

I ignored that. "Where have you been since brunch? Making snow angels?" I asked, noting that his clothes weren't exactly fresh out of the dryer. I guess I still had laundry on the brain.

"Some of the guys invited me to play a little pickup game of football on the Green."

"Oh?" I smirked. "Taking this whole prep school boy persona pretty seriously, huh?"

"What can I say? Cover is cover."

"That reminds me. Part of my cover is taking Mr. Keep-Away here for walksies. And we're late." I grabbed Killer's leash and snapped it to the collar. This time he didn't protest. Probably didn't want to look bad in front of Frank.

"I'll come along." Frank fell into step as we left the cottage. "We need to talk."

My mind immediately jumped to the mission. "Did you hear from HQ about the lab results?"

Frank shook his head as we turned down our usual path near the woods. "Not yet. But there's more trouble. Nigel Nabb just showed up on campus."

"Nigel Nabb?" It took me a second to place the name. "Wait, you mean that big-mouthed Brit that Aunt Trudy's always pretending not to watch on TV while she cleans?"

"That's the one," Frank confirmed. "I think his show's called *R and F Report*."

"Right. Stands for 'rich and famous.'"

R and F Report was a weekly tabloid-trash cable show that focused on celebrity gossip. It was pretty popular, though I wasn't sure why. Watching its star reporter, Nigel Nabb, was about as annoying as having a mosquito in your swim trunks. He was known for exposé-type reports that he produced on location. A lot of his footage was shot with a handheld camera. Guess he thought it gave him that cinema verité look.

Frank and I had seen way more of the show than we wanted to. Aunt Trudy, who lives with us, always seemed to have it on while she vacuumed or fixed dinner. Whenever anyone caught her watching, she pretended she'd been flipping channels trying to find PBS or the Weather Channel.

"So what's someone like Nigel Nabb doing at a place like this?" I asked.

Frank shrugged. "Spencer and some of the other guys tell me the show loves to focus on scandals among socialites and rich club kids and people like that. Not just the typical movie-star-type celebs."

"Think old Nigel heard about any of what's been going on around here lately?"

"Maybe. Or maybe he's just sniffing around

for a prep school story and the timing is a coincidence." Frank kicked at a loose stone on the path. "Either way, let's hope Darity chases this clown off soon."

I nodded. "This investigation's already way too complicated. The last thing we need is some nosy reporter getting in the way."

Frank's phone buzzed. It turned out to be HQ reporting those lab results. The Winner's Cup had been laced with a certain anticonvulsant drug normally used to treat epilepsy and related conditions. But in a way high dose.

"Good thing there were two MVPs," Frank said as he hung up. "If one person had drunk that much in a single gulp, he might not have recovered so quickly and easily."

"Or she," I reminded him. "Think this was a leftover swipe at Destiny?"

"Doubtful. Casey thought he was taking her out of the game, remember? He'd have had no reason to think she'd even be around to drink out of that cup."

"Good point." I tugged at Killer's leash to move him past a fascinating splotch of bird poop. "So how hard would it be for someone to get their hands on a drug like that?"

"It's prescription only. But not particularly

obscure," said Frank. "Any doctor could get it. Or any diagnosed epileptic, I guess."

That didn't seem too helpful. So we went back to our previous conversation. Frank told me what Nigel's unwelcome arrival had interrupted. A near fight on the Green.

"Wow," I said when I heard about the rumor that had started the scuffle. "They're claiming Lee poisoned *himself*? That's so obviously not true. It doesn't even make sense."

"I know," Frank said. "I wonder who started it."

"Didn't you say it was Peachy?" That was Patton's nickname, thanks to his red hair.

"He was the one who told those guys. But I doubt he came up with it himself." Frank looked thoughtful. "I wonder if it has anything to do with Nigel turning up?"

I caught his meaning immediately. "It does seem pretty coincidental," I said.

I didn't pay much attention to *R and F Report*. But it was hard to avoid hearing the rumors that the show exaggerated or even downright fabricated some of its juicier stories.

"I guess all we can do is keep the possibility in mind," said Frank. "Meanwhile, we'd better get back to the real mission."

"Agreed. So where do we start?"

"Let's go over the facts so far, see if we can spot any patterns."

That was typical Frank. He's all about focusing on details and making lists and looking for patterns. Me? I'm more of a big-picture, action kind of guy. But in this case, he was on target. There were a few loose ends we hadn't tied up even before the Winner's Cup incident. Were we missing something?

Spotting our favorite trail leading into the forest, I turned down it. Less chance of being overheard in there. Plus, I didn't have to clean up Killer's poop if he went in the woods.

"Okay," I said. "Ellery claimed he didn't know anything about some of the early computer threats."

"We never figured out who greased the coach's floor, either."

"Right. I almost forgot about that one." Before our arrival on campus, the school's swim coach had been badly injured when he'd slipped on some grease on the soccer coach's office floor. "Guess I just figured it was a coincidence."

"Me too. Same with Lee's grades getting changed in the computer system."

"What about the buckets of blood and the graffiti?" I automatically shot a glance in the direction of the hunting cabin where we'd found that blood.

It was tucked away in the woods near campus. "Casey said he didn't do it."

"I know." Frank looked troubled. "I kind of didn't believe him at first. But now that I think about it, how would he get his hands on Destiny's blood supply?"

He had a point. Destiny had a rare blood type and an even rarer blood-clotting disorder. She had to keep a supply of her own blood on hand in case of emergency.

"He might have known about Destiny's stash from going to school with her before," I said. "Could he have broken into the infirmary here to grab it?"

"I suppose it's possible. But we shouldn't assume anything." Frank shrugged. "I mean, he confessed to everything else. Why not that one thing?"

"He didn't confess to trying to run her down with that truck on the soccer field, either," I reminded him. "That could've killed Destiny if a certain heroic ATAC agent hadn't come to the rescue." I grinned, remembering how Frank had leaped into the truck to steer it away from Destiny.

"Shh!" Frank looked worried as he quickly surveyed the woods around us. "Half the people on campus already know about ATAC as it is. You don't have to announce it to the other half."

"Who do you think is going to overhear us out here? The squirrels?" But again, I had to admit he had a point. We had circled back to the edge of the woods by now. I followed Killer as he pulled me out into the sun.

"Whatever. Anyway, who was hurt by all that stuff?" Frank asked quietly, checking around to make sure nobody was nearby. "Who might have a motive?"

I paused to let Killer do his business on the side of a trash can. "Who was hurt?" I mused. "All different people. The swim coach. Lee. Destiny. Anyone else?"

We kept discussing it as we wandered through campus. We were just crossing behind fraternity row when Frank's phone rang. Killer instantly went on alert, ears pricked toward Frank's pocket.

"At ease, soldier," Frank told the dog with a smile. Then he grabbed his phone and answered it. His face immediately went pale. "Oh, um, h-hi, Aunt Trudy," he stammered.

I gulped. Aunt Trudy is kind of a barracuda. She's always after Frank and me—well, mostly me—to finish our homework, do our chores, that kind of stuff. Basically, if we're in any danger of having fun, she puts a stop to it.

And she has no idea about ATAC. Neither does

our mom. Dad knows, of course. He's the only reason Frank and I have been able to keep the secret. He and ATAC help us come up with cover stories to explain why we have to spend so much time away from home.

Sometimes the stories are a little weak. Like the current one. Supposedly we were involved in a school exchange program. We'd left it to Dad to come up with the details after we left.

The campus around us was pretty quiet. Aunt Trudy's voice isn't. I was able to hear her pretty well even from several feet away with a large dog panting at my side. She was squawking about all the chores we weren't doing at home. Your basic guilt trip.

"Sorry about that, Aunt Trudy," Frank broke in at last, using his best straight-A, Eagle Scout voice. "But our educational exchange program is going very well. And we'll be sure to take care of Playback's cages just as soon as we get home."

Ugh. I'd almost forgotten about our pet parrot's cages. We were supposed to clean them right before we left on this mission.

But I was distracted from that unpleasant thought by Killer. He was pulling on the leash, straining ahead toward the next corner.

"Hush!" I whispered as he started whining softly.

As usual, he paid no attention to me. He let out a loud *WOOOOF!*

Aunt Trudy's voice came through more clearly than ever. "What's that noise?' she demanded. "Are you at a school or a dog show?"

Frank grimaced. "Um, they're showing a filmstrip in the next room," he said. "I think it's about . . . uh, the use of military dogs during World War II."

Nicely done. But I barely had time to appreciate his quick lying skills. Killer was dragging me around the bend.

That's when I saw it. Two students on the GTT house lawn, trying to kill each other!

Fratricide

I managed to rush Aunt Trudy off the phone. Then I sprinted after Joe. He was already trying to break up the fight. Killer was dancing around, barking.

"Chill out, man!" Joe yelled, grabbing at one kid's arm.

I lunged toward the other. It was Van.

"Hey!" I shouted. "Easy, big guy!"

By now others had heard the yells. Several guys ran out of the frat house. Spencer was one of them.

Soon the fighters were backing off. Spencer was holding on to Van's arms, talking softly to calm him down. Killer had placed himself between the two fighters and was keeping a wary eye on both of them.

Van's opponent, a small, wiry guy with dark hair, brushed himself off. He still looked kind of tense.

"Who's that?" Joe whispered to me.

"Name's Tommy. Tommy Lewicki, I think— something like that," I murmured back. "Lee pointed him out to me once. Said he's a freshman from the same Boston public school as him."

"Another scholarship student?"

"Guess so. The way Lee was talking, it sounded like he sees him as sort of a little brother here, you know?"

"Okay," Spencer was saying to the fighters. "We cool now, guys?"

Van was starting to look kind of sheepish. No wonder. He had to outweigh Tommy by at least fifty pounds.

"Sorry, bro," he said. "Guess I just got upset."

Another GTT brother let out a laugh. "Hothead Van strikes again," he joked.

"Yeah." Van grinned. "Anyway, I just heard the latest rumors about why Ellery left school, and after the stuff Peachy told us earlier, well . . ." He shrugged.

"Wait, what rumors about Ellery?" Joe asked, stepping forward.

Van blinked at him, obviously not quite sure who he was. A few of the other GTTers traded glances. Finally Spencer cleared his throat.

"What was it this time, Van?" he asked quietly.

Van shrugged. "I heard Lee got his girlfriend Destiny to say that Ellery was, like, harassing her or something. That way Ell would get kicked out, and Lee would get into GTT for sure."

"Crazy, huh?" Tommy spoke up, sounding angry and a little on edge.

Crazy was right. Mr. Marks had hushed up the truth so well that not even Ellery's closest friends knew the truth. Except for Spencer, of course. And apparently, he hadn't shared with his frat brothers.

Spencer rolled his eyes. "Come on, man," he chided Van. "That story doesn't jive. Lee and Ellery were both getting in."

A few of the others nodded, including Van. But a couple of brothers didn't look convinced.

"I dunno," one said. "Lee's pretty new to Firth, just like his girlfriend. Neither of them really fits in, you know?"

Tommy instantly clenched his fists. "What do you mean by that?" he challenged him.

"Chill, dude!" another brother said. "He's just saying—"

The rest of his words were lost in a flurry of barking. I glanced over to see Joe struggling to hang on to Killer's leash. The dog was straining toward something off to one side of the house.

"Oh, man," one of the brothers muttered. "It's that gossip guy."

Sure enough, Killer had spotted Nigel Nabb coming our way. The reporter was holding his camera and microphone. He was still in his shiny suit, though he'd added a scarf sporting Firth's school colors somewhere along the way. It looked ridiculous nestled among his chest hair.

Most news spread fast at Firth. Nigel's arrival was no exception. Everyone seemed to recognize him instantly, and nobody looked surprised.

"Relax, guys," Spencer hissed. "When he gets here, we were just arguing about this year's Celtics lineup or something, okay?"

"Says who?" Tommy spoke up with a frown. "Maybe if you guys don't believe Lee is innocent, that reporter dude can help clear his name."

"Are you psycho?" One of the GTT brothers shot a nervous look at Nigel, who was getting closer. "My cousin ended up on that *R and F* show once, and she's barely been able to show her face in public since. Nabb will rip Firth apart if he gets half a chance."

"He's right," said Spencer. "Whatever our issues are, let's deal with them ourselves and not go spouting off to outsiders. Firth First, remember?"

That was the school's unofficial motto. Firth First.

Tommy shrugged, looking sullen. "Whatever," he muttered. "Guess you're right."

Killer had stopped barking by now. But he was still glaring at Nigel. Guess he didn't like gossip TV, either. Smart dog.

"Come on," Joe said to me. "Maybe we should get out of here."

I nodded and led the way around the corner of the frat house. The less time we spent with Nigel Nabb, the better. If he was looking for prep school secrets, we definitely didn't want him to uncover ours.

Once we were safely out of sight—and Killer was settled down and sniffing at some fallen leaves—Joe and I huddled to talk about what had just happened.

"Think it means anything?" he asked.

"I don't know," I replied. "But I'm thinking we should talk to Lee. Even though all the rumors about him are bogus, he does seem to be at the center of things lately."

We tried calling him, but there was no answer.

I remembered that he'd been at his work-study job in the campus office the previous Sunday. But when we checked there, his coworkers said he had the day off. We already knew he wasn't at the frat house, so we headed for his dorm room.

"Wait, we didn't talk about what we're going to say," I whispered as Joe raised a hand to knock on Lee's door.

He shrugged. "We'll figure it out. We always do."

Typical. But it was too late to protest. He rapped sharply on the door.

The hall was deserted and quiet. It was easy to hear a couple of thumps from inside the room. Killer even pricked his ears in that direction. Then everything went silent.

"Lee?" Joe called. "You okay in there, bro?"

Still no answer. We traded a confused look.

"Am I crazy, or did you hear someone in there?" I asked.

"I thought so." Joe carefully tested the knob. Locked. He looked quickly up and down the empty hallway. "Think we should bust in?"

I hesitated. If Lee was in there and just didn't feel like company, it would be hard to explain if we forced our way into his room. . . .

The sound of voices and footsteps made up our

minds for us. "Come on," I murmured to Joe as some other students appeared farther down the hall. "We'll check back later."

"Okay." Joe shot a look back at Lee's locked door. "But that was kind of weird. I'm thinking it might be time to put Lee back on the suspect list."

We'd already had HQ pull a dossier on Lee, but I texted them to see if they'd turned up anything else.

SUSPECT PROFILE

Name: Lee Jenkins

Hometown: Boston, Massachusetts

Physical description: 6'1", 180 pounds, prominent nose and crooked teeth, but handsome in an offbeat way

Occupation: Junior at Firth; scholarship student who transferred at beginning of the year; GTT pledge, soon to be brother; star soccer player

Suspicious behavior: Sneaking around with Destiny Darity; possibly hiding out in his room; has a lot of rumors flying about him.

Then Joe and I headed back toward his cottage. Since he was posing as a school employee, he got his own little place near the rest of the staff. We'd have plenty of privacy there to talk over how to proceed.

Halfway there, we got a call from Dr. Darity. He wanted us to come to his office and fill him in on our progress.

"Think we have time to drop off you-know-who first?" Joe asked.

I smiled and shook my head. Joe is always trying to ditch Killer. Maybe that's why the dog isn't that crazy about him.

"Sorry, bro. Darity sounded impatient—we'd better head straight there."

"Are you sure? Darity's allergic to dogs, remember? That's why Killer doesn't live with him."

"I know. But he's been around him before.

I don't think having him sit in his office for five minutes is going to kill him."

A few minutes later we were in Darity's office in Firth Hall. First we told him the lab results.

"So it was nothing illegal? Just a prescription drug?" Darity stroked his chin. As usual, he looked tweedy and a little rumpled. In other words, exactly how you'd expect the headmaster of an exclusive prep school to look.

"That's right," said Joe. "But listen, there's something else you should know about. Have you heard that Nigel Nabb is hanging around?"

"Who?" Darity blinked at us over the tops of his little round glasses.

"Nigel Nabb," I said. Guessing that Darity didn't spend much time watching *R and F Report*, I quickly gave him the 411 on the guy. "He's been poking around campus for at least the past hour or so," I added.

"I see." Darity looked concerned but not too alarmed. "Well, we do get the odd gossip reporter up here now and then. No wonder, given that our student body comes from some of the most esteemed names on the Forbes 500. I'll look into it."

"Good idea," I said. "Because if he figures out what's been going on—"

Darity's phone rang, cutting me off. Like almost everything else in the office, it was old-fashioned and dusty.

"Excuse me, fellows," Darity said as he reached for it. "Unless there's anything else . . ."

Joe and I stood. "Nothing important," I said. "We'll keep you posted, sir."

We grabbed Killer and headed for the door. As we opened it, the dog's hackles rose and he let out a growl.

"Easy, boy," said Joe. "What are you—oh."

We'd both just spotted Nigel Nabb. He was scuttling down the dim, dusty hallway, heading away from Darity's office door.

He turned around when he realized he'd been spotted. "Hullo, chaps. Fascinating old building, isn't it? Just getting some location shots." He patted his camera and flashed us an ingratiating smile.

Joe narrowed his eyes. "Location shots, huh?" he said. "Isn't it a little dark in here for that?"

"Oh, you'd be amazed by what today's technology can do." Nigel's smile never wavered. The guy was good.

I looked nervously at the microphone he was holding. Today's technology indeed. The thing was so high-tech it made the space shuttle look like a paper airplane. Exactly how sensitive was it? Sensitive enough to, say, pick up on a couple of ATAC agents' voices through some thick old walls?

"Come on," I said to Joe. "Let's get out of here."

We headed for the exit. Killer kept tossing suspicious glances back at Nigel. I knew how he felt.

"That was interesting," Joe said as soon as we emerged onto the steps outside. "Think he heard anyth—"

KA-BOOOOM! The rest of his comment was swallowed up in an ear-shattering explosion from somewhere close by.

Weird Science

"**C**ome on!" I yelled, taking the steps three at a time. "That came from the direction of the frat houses!"

Killer was ahead of me, and Frank right at my heels. We raced down the alley between Firth Hall and the next building. That brought us in view of fraternity row—and the huge smoking hole in the lawn in front of the GTT house!

"Whoa," said Frank. "Wasn't there a tree there?"

"*Was* being the operative word," I said.

We rushed over. GTT brothers were pouring out of the house. Most of them looked pretty shaken. No wonder. It's not every day half your front yard explodes.

"What was that?" one of the guys shouted.

Spencer was staring at the pile of matchsticks that had once been a tree. "Oh, man!" he exclaimed.

There was a moment of chaos. People were running around, shouting. One or two of them appeared to be bleeding. The explosion must have blown out some windows in the house.

Meanwhile I was having problems of my own. Killer kept lunging off to one side of the yard, away from the ex-tree. Since he was a former police dog, I knew he'd been trained to sniff out explosives and stuff. He'd proved that by locating a bomb that Ellery had planted. So why was he acting like he wanted to get away from the scene of the crime?

"Knock it off!" I yelled, yanking on his leash.

I wanted to check out the explosion site before any clues or evidence got trampled by the students milling around. But the dog refused to give up. I gritted my teeth, wishing I'd ignored Frank and taken the beast home before the meeting with Darity.

Killer barked loudly and lunged away again. This time he pulled me off balance a little. That was all the opening he needed. He took off toward the evergreen hedge between the GTT house and the next place over. I scuttled a few steps after him, desperate to keep my hold on his leash. The last thing I wanted was to have him get loose and end up chasing him all over campus. Been there, done that.

"Quit it, you mangy . . . huh?"

I blinked as Killer skidded to a stop and barked again. His long, narrow nose was pointing to something sticking out from under the hedge. It was a plastic bag with some stuff spilling out of it. Some suspicious-looking stuff.

I moved aside slightly to block it from view. Then I looked around for Frank. He was nearby questioning a couple of the brothers. They seemed shaken as they insisted they had no idea what had happened.

Ducking down, I glanced into the bag. Just as I'd thought. ATAC had given us some basic explosives training. More than enough to recognize the remains of a simple chemical setup for a home-made bomb.

"Killer, sit," I told the dog. "Stay."

Killer sank to his haunches, his ears pricked in my direction. For once he seemed willing to take orders from me. I just hoped it wasn't a trick. But I had to take the chance. Dropping his leash, I hoped for the best.

Whew! He seemed willing to stay put. His furry body was in front of the bag, hiding it from view.

Frank was still talking with the brothers. Dashing past him, I headed for Spencer. He was standing alone, staring into the crater the bomb had left in the yard.

"Dude," I hissed to him. "Can you get everyone back inside for a few?"

Spencer caught on fast. He knew Frank and I were with ATAC. "You got it," he murmured.

Within minutes all the brothers were filing back into the house, along with a few random people who had heard the explosion and come to see what was happening. It was pretty impressive. Frank looked a little confused as Spencer herded them all inside like a border collie rounding up the flock.

Meanwhile I was making a beeline for Killer. "Check this out," I called over my shoulder.

Frank's eyes widened when he saw what was behind the dog. He bent to examine the contents of the bag. "Whoa," he said.

"Let's pack it up and get out of here." I glanced at the frat house. "With any luck, maybe the culprit left some fingerprints somewhere."

"Okay." Frank pulled some thin latex gloves out of his pocket, along with a plastic bag. "But I'm not holding my breath."

"Me either. But hurry, let's move before anyone starts asking questions."

Soon we were back in my cottage. Killer was lounging in his kennel while Frank and I took a closer look at the contents of the bag. "No doubt this stuff was used to make that bomb," said Frank, sitting back on the sofa and peeling off his gloves. "But it could've come from any decently stocked science classroom."

I nodded. As expected, there were no fingerprints to be found. Or anything else to tell us who the bomb maker might be. Even the plastic bag was generic, a recycled number from the school store.

"So now what?" I said.

Frank looked thoughtful. "Let's think for a minute. Who was at the frat house when it went off?"

I shrugged. "Usual suspects," I said. "Spencer, the other frat guys, the new pledges—well, not all of them." I stopped to think for a minute. "I don't remember seeing Lee around. Or Patton, either."

"Patton wouldn't be," Frank pointed out. "He got cut again, remember? Or at least everyone assumes he's going to be."

"Oh, right. Makes sense he wouldn't be hanging around then. Poor Peachy—rejected two years in a row." I glanced at Frank. "Think he's taking out his disappointment on GTT?"

"I guess it's possible." Frank stared at the bomb-making stuff spread before us. "We already suspected he might have been the one who tampered with Lee's grades, trying to make him look bad. He could have done some of the other stuff too, I suppose."

"Or he could have done this but *not* the other stuff." I kicked back and put my feet up on the coffee table. "After all, we've already nabbed two bad guys on this mission so far. Why shouldn't there be three or four more to go?"

Frank groaned. "Don't even say that! Anyway, I think it's worth adding Patton back onto the list."

"No argument there, bro."

SUSPECT PROFILE

<u>Name</u>: Patton "Peachy" Gage

<u>Hometown</u>: Miami, Florida

<u>Physical description</u>: 5'9", 155 pounds, pale skin, red hair, freckles, currently sporting acid-burned skin on his face

<u>Occupation</u>: Junior at Firth; two-time GTT rejectee

<u>Suspicious behavior</u>: Spreading gossip about Lee.

<u>Suspected of</u>: Planting bomb at GTT house; possibly other incidents.

Frank checked his watch. "Let's not just sit around here," he said. "When Aunt Trudy called today, she was sounding kind of . . ."

"Aunt Trudyish?" I supplied.

Frank grimaced. "Yeah. Anyway, the faster we wrap things up here, the better. She and Mom are going to start getting suspicious if we miss another week of school back home."

He had a point. "So what do you have in mind?" I asked. "Want to check out the science lab, see if anyone noticed anybody sneaking around there this weekend?"

"Why don't you do that?" Frank said. "I was thinking of digging into the school's computer records, see if we can find out which students or faculty might have access to that drug that was in the Winner's Cup."

Computer research sounded pretty boring to me. In other words, right up Frank's alley.

"Okay, let's split up." I jumped to my feet. "Science lab, here I come."

"What about Killer?" Frank reminded me as I was heading for the door. "You might want to take him along. You know, as cover."

I groaned. If Frank had his way, that dog would be glued to my side 24/7.

But he had a point. It was easier to blend in when Killer was with me—nobody asked questions if I went just about anywhere as long as he was there too. The dog was seriously popular around campus.

Besides, I couldn't help remembering how Killer had zeroed right in on those bomb-making supplies. Maybe he'd come in handy again. Hey, you never know.

The science center was a lot more modern than most of the buildings at Firth. In other words, it had actually been constructed during this century. It was mostly concrete and green-tinted glass. Tasteful pewter letters spelled out the name MARKS SCIENCE CENTER over the doorway.

Yeah, Marks. As in Ellery. The kid's family was loaded, and they weren't shy about showing it off. Their name was all over Firth on various buildings, plaques, and trophies.

And they weren't the only ones. The building right next door housed the school's indoor pool. It was labeled the Lewis McPherson Sr. Swimming Complex. Lewis McPherson *Jr.* was the kid who'd been killed when one of Ellery's pranks went awry. Now here his name was, right next door to his killer's.

"Ironic, huh?" I murmured to Killer.

The dog shot me a bored glance. I shrugged and headed into the science building. He padded along beside me.

The place was empty and echoing. No surprise, since it was Sunday. Luckily, nothing was locked. I started poking around to see which classrooms held the supplies in question.

When I opened the third or fourth door, I was surprised to find someone inside. I was even more surprised to realize it was Dr. Montgomery.

"Hello, my boy," the former headmaster said in his quavery old-man voice, looking up from some test tubes. "Can I help you?"

"Um . . ." Like Spencer, Dr. Montgomery knew that Frank and I were with ATAC. However, I wasn't sure I wanted to remind him of that fact. Maybe he was senile enough to have forgotten. "Just taking Killer for a walk. But what are you doing here?"

"Didn't you know, son?" Dr. Montgomery smiled. "I still teach a senior science seminar for the more . . . worthy seniors here at Firth."

"Oh." As a matter of fact, I *hadn't* known that. But I didn't much care, either. It wasn't exactly the info I'd been looking for.

"As long as you're here, my boy, could you help me with something?" The old man pointed to one of the windows along one wall of the lab. "I wanted to open that window to allow this place to air out a bit, but it's a little sticky, and I'm afraid my old back isn't up to the task."

"Sure." I stepped over and yanked the window open. "By the way, Doc, have you noticed anything missing from your lab the past day or two?"

"Missing? What do you mean?"

What the heck? He already knew, right? I made an executive decision, figuring Frank would understand. Maybe.

"There was an explosion outside the GTT house," I said. "Nobody was hurt, but we're trying to track down how it happened."

I figured that was a good compromise. I hadn't actually reminded Montgomery about the ATAC stuff. If he remembered on his own, well, no biggie, since we already knew that he knew.

Dr. Montgomery looked startled as I went on to list the chemicals and stuff we'd found. "As a matter of fact, I did notice just today that I seem to be missing a few things," he said, glancing at a wall of open shelving that held a bunch of vials and beakers full of various liquids and powders. "I thought I'd just misplaced or mislabeled them, but perhaps . . ."

"Have you seen anyone sneaking around this place in the past couple of days?" I asked. "Especially anyone connected with GTT?"

"Oh, I'm sure those boys would never pull such a serious and dangerous prank." Montgomery shook his head firmly, then hesitated. "Well, *most* of them, in any case . . ."

He looked troubled. I was about to ask him what he meant by "*most* of them."

But before I could, I heard a piercing, terrified scream from somewhere outside that open window.

Sneaky Dealings

"I don't know, Frank." Dr. Darity looked concerned. He glanced at the computer on his desk. "The Firth community's medical information is always kept strictly confidential. Perhaps I can have the medical staff check into the stored drug supplies and get back to me. I can pretend it's just a routine inventory or something."

"I'd really rather not wait that long, sir," I said, doing my best to hide my impatience. "We need to know who poisoned that Winner's Cup—the sooner the better. Otherwise the culprit might strike again."

Darity still seemed hesitant. I got that. He seemed like an upright guy for the most part, and he obviously took his job seriously. But this could be a matter of life and death.

"You don't have to worry," I assured him. "ATAC will keep any information we find strictly confidential."

Darity checked his watch, looking harried. He'd already mentioned he was about to leave for a late luncheon with some trustees. "I need to head out before I'm late, and my secretary doesn't come in on Sundays," he said. "Maybe we should meet first thing tomorrow and take care of this, hmm?"

"I'd really rather handle it today, if you don't mind," I said firmly as he stood up. "But if you need to leave, that's fine. I'm pretty handy with a computer. All I need is for you to type in the necessary passwords or whatever and I can take it from there."

For a moment Darity looked ready to argue. But then he checked his watch again and sighed.

"Fine," he said. "As long as I have your personal assurance that the information goes no further than ATAC personnel. If the outside world got hold of some of it . . ."

"Absolutely. You can count on us, sir."

He stared at me for a long moment. I just sat there, doing my best to look trustworthy and responsible.

Anyway, he finally bent over the keyboard for a moment, then straightened up. "There you go," he said. "You should be able to access whatever you need. Please log off when you're finished, all right?"

"Of course. Thank you, sir. And enjoy your luncheon."

Darity just grimaced. I wasn't sure if he was dreading the luncheon for some reason, or already regretting giving me access to the school records. Either way, he just gave me a little wave, grabbed his coat from behind the door, and left.

Within seconds I was searching the medical records. It turned out there were several people at Firth with a history of epilepsy or related conditions. One of the arts teachers, a couple of students whose names I didn't recognize . . . and one whose name I definitely *did*.

"Zeke?" I murmured, blinking at the name on the screen in surprise. "Whoa."

Zeke was my roommate. Not that he was too happy about that. In fact, he'd made it pretty clear all along that he resented losing his private room when I showed up. He definitely wasn't the type to hold back on his opinions. Or his burps or various other bodily emissions either, as I'd learned being his roommate.

"Guess old Zeke's just full of surprises," I

mumbled to myself, remembering that he'd recently won an award for poetry. Trust me, if you met Zeke, poetry would be the last thing you'd expect to come out of him.

After making a quick mental note of all the relevant names, I clicked away from the medical info page. Then I glanced at the door, realizing I had a unique opportunity for a little extracurricular snooping.

See, Joe and I liked Darity. Like I said, he came across as a stand-up guy. But more than once, we'd had to wonder if the headmaster was being totally straight with us. We'd caught him in a few minor lies over the course of the investigation, mostly of omission. Nothing major, but still . . .

Clicking over to Darity's desktop, I scanned the file folders there. Most of them were pretty boring stuff—financial records, admissions reports, that kind of thing.

There were also a bunch of folders detailing various plans for modernizing the school. Darity had been headmaster for only a few years, but he'd already made lots of changes at Firth and was planning more. Some were welcome, like computerizing the records. Others were more controversial, like the persistent rumor that he wanted to do away with the fraternity system. Could those plans make someone angry enough to lash out?

A quick look through the folders didn't turn up anything suspicious. At least not until I came across a subfolder labeled "Love Letters." I almost clicked right past that one, figuring that sort of thing was none of my business.

Then I hesitated, my mind flashing to Darity's daughter Destiny. What if this had something to do with her relationship with Lee? Everyone thought Lee was one of Darity's personal favorites, the shining success of his new scholarship program. But what if the headmaster didn't like the idea of a poor kid dating his own daughter? He didn't seem like the type, but you never knew at a place like this. . . .

Feeling a bit uneasy, I opened the folder, ready to click away again if I found only a bunch of romantic e-mails between Darity and whoever.

But it was nothing like that at all. The folder was packed with dozens of angry e-mails from alumni. Most of them were complaints about the changes Darity had made since taking over.

I scanned a few of them. Some of the writers seemed *really* angry.

Was this a clue? The complaint letters certainly brought up a motive we hadn't thought about much. Could one of these irate alums be trying to make Darity look bad in order to push him out?

I was still pondering that when I noticed another file. It was tucked away in the corner between a couple of boring ones, so I hadn't spotted it at first. It was labeled BoE.

"Brothers of Erebus?" I breathed, clicking on it.

Sure enough, the mysterious secret society's name was spelled out on a couple of the documents inside. I checked around, but there wasn't much to see. There was a map of the tunnels under the school. The tunnel system had been long forgotten by everyone except the Brothers of Erebus. We'd recently discovered that the group was still using them to sneak around and perform their rituals.

There were also lists of current and recently graduated students who were BoE members. I scanned the names, seeing no huge surprises. Spencer was there, of course, along with several other senior GTT brothers. Lee's name was at the bottom of the list of current students.

That was about it. Nothing we didn't already know from ATAC's research. But even the crack team at HQ hadn't been able to turn up much more than this. The BoE really put the "secret" in "secret society."

I sat there, staring at the computer screen. When we'd busted Ellery, Darity had claimed to know nothing about the Brothers of Erebus. He'd looked as shocked as anyone to hear of the group's very existence.

Was he telling the truth? Had he created this folder after that? Or was he still lying to us?

SUSPECT PROFILE

Name: Dr. Robert Darity

Physical description: 6'0", 180 pounds, brown hair, hazel eyes, glasses

Occupation: Headmaster of Firth Academy (approx. four years)

Suspicious behavior: Has hidden information in the past; has info on Brothers of Erebus on computer though claimed he knew nothing about the group.

Suspected of: Knowing more than he lets on about the trouble on campus.

Possible motives: Trying to break up Destiny and Lee; possibly trying to push through his modernizing changes faster; other possible motives unknown at this time.

I was about to forward the whole BoE folder to ATAC HQ when I heard the sound of rushed footsteps in the hallway outside the office. Uh-oh. It was probably Darity returning to check on me. Or maybe someone stopping by to drop something off, or a member of the cleaning staff or something.

Clicking away from the incriminating BoE folder, I opened my mouth to call out a cheerful (and totally innocent-sounding) greeting.

But something made me hold back. Maybe it was the slow, careful way the door started to glide open. Holding my tongue, I dove behind one of the long, dusty curtains on the windows at the back of the room.

Just in time. Lee Jenkins stuck his head into the office and glanced around. I stayed where I was, frozen with surprise.

Lee didn't see me. Darting into the room, he scrabbled around near the coatrack. Then he ducked out again just as quickly, pulling the door shut behind him.

I waited until I was sure he was gone. Then I emerged from my hiding place and hurried over to see what he'd been doing.

Right next to the coatrack was a key rack. And judging by the dust spot on the wall, I was pretty sure that Lee had just taken one of the keys.

Sink or Swim

"**W**hat are you doing, young man?" Dr. Montgomery called out, sounding confused. I vaulted through the open lab window. Killer jumped out after me. Explanations would have to wait. That scream had come from somewhere close by. As soon as I got outside, I realized where. The pool complex. It was right across a narrow alley from here.

Sprinting over there, I let myself and the dog in through the closest door. That put us in the main lobby. The whole place smelled like chlorine.

The filters hummed from the direction of the lap pool, visible through an open doorway off to the left. But the scream had come from the other direction.

I pushed through a door on that side and found myself in a hallway leading to the locker rooms. Destiny Darity was standing there. She was dressed in a sporty one-piece swimsuit. A damp towel was wrapped around her torso.

Even with that towel covering most of the interesting parts, I was so distracted by the sight of her in a bathing suit that it took me a few seconds to realize that she was the one who'd screamed. She wasn't screaming anymore, though. Now she was standing there, yelling at someone. Nigel Nabb. Killer let out a low growl as he sank to his haunches beside me.

". . . and if that's the kind of so-called story you go for, you're an even bigger loser than you seem on TV!" Destiny was shouting. Spotting me, she whirled around, her eyes spitting fire. Based on her expression, I guessed she was expecting me to be one of Nigel's backup cameramen or someone.

"Hi," I said mildly. "Something wrong here?"

"Yeah—him!" Destiny jabbed a finger in Nigel's direction. "Can you believe this creep? He sneaked into the locker room and started filming while I was getting ready to change after my swim. Pathetic!"

She turned and spat the last word right into Nigel's face. He kept right on smiling, aiming his camera at her.

"Care to repeat that, sweetheart?" he said in his smarmy accent. "I'd love to get a better angle on your face this time."

Destiny responded with a few words I was pretty sure weren't allowed on TV. Not even cable.

I didn't blame her for being a little on edge. It couldn't be easy being her these days. She'd had her blood supply stolen. Been burned in effigy. Almost been run over. Nearly been poisoned. And finally found out that someone she'd thought was her friend had done most of it.

That reminded me. I was supposed to be trying to figure out who'd been responsible for the rest of it. But first I needed to defuse this situation. Otherwise I had the feeling Destiny would soon be adding to the campus body count by strangling Nigel with her bare hands.

"Look, I'm sure this is just a misunderstanding, right?" I said, trying to channel Frank's best Mr. Diplomat tone.

"Of course it was," said Nigel, still sporting that fake-looking smile. "This young lady was swimming alone and I was concerned, that's all. After all that's been going on at Firth Academy lately, it wouldn't do for the headmaster's daughter to come to any harm, would it?"

I was careful to keep my expression neutral. So Nigel knew there'd been some recent trouble on campus, huh? Interesting.

"Well, she seems to be all right," I said. "So how about deleting whatever footage you have of her and calling it a day?"

"How about *not*." Nigel's smile morphed into a smirk. "This camera is private property. So is any footage that might happen to be on it."

"Oh, yeah? Well my hands are *my* private property," Destiny countered. "And if I can get them on *your* private property, it's not going to be pretty."

I could only hope she was still talking about the camera. Either way, things were really getting tense.

Then I remembered something. I had a secret weapon right there at my side. Killer.

"Look, Mr. Nabb. We've tried being reasonable, but you're making it difficult," I said in as James Bond a manner as I could. Then I glanced down at the dog. "Isn't that right, Killer?"

For once Killer seemed to catch on to what I wanted. And more surprisingly, to go along with it. He let out an impressive growl and took a step toward Nigel, his eyes locked on the man's ruddy face.

"Hey, hey, now, kids." Nigel immediately sounded a lot less smug. "Let's not do anything we'll regret here. . . ."

He was watching Killer carefully. That was all the opening I needed. Jumping forward, I grabbed the camera right out of his hand.

"Hey!" he shouted, lunging after me.

But Killer stopped him in his tracks with a loud, commanding bark. Nigel jumped back again. Killer's hackles were up. He looked pretty scary.

Destiny wasn't paying any attention to the dog. "Give me that camera," she exclaimed. "I want to throw it in the pool!"

"That shouldn't be necessary."

I spun around as she danced around me, poking me—hard—in the shoulders and trying to snatch the camera out of my hands. Good thing my ATAC training taught me to multitask. And to work almost any piece of electronic equipment out there. Nigel's camera was pretty standard issue. Within seconds I'd erased everything on the memory card.

And yeah, I was good. I didn't even try to peek.

"There we go. All gone," I said, dodging Destiny. "Heads up, pal."

I tossed the camera in Nigel's direction. He

scrabbled for it, barely managing to keep it from falling to the hard tile floor.

"Are you mad?" he snapped. "That's an expensive piece of equipment! Then again, I suppose you prep-school brats wouldn't know anything about what things cost."

"Shows how much you know, loser," Destiny told him. "He's not a student. He's just the school dog walker."

"Is that so?" Nigel shot me a very unpleasant look. "Well, I hope that gig pays you enough to retain a good attorney. Because I won't have anyone messing with my livelihood. Not to mention the public's right to know."

"Since when does the public have the right to know what color underwear Destiny's wearing?" I challenged him.

Nigel let out a curse and took a quick step toward me, his hands clenched. But Killer blocked him, punctuating the move with a low growl.

"Never mind. You're not worth it," Nigel spat out. "But you haven't seen the last of me, mate. Count on it." He whirled on the heel of his expensive-looking loafer and stomped off.

"Good work, boy," I told Killer with a smile. Then I glanced at Destiny. "You okay?"

She shrugged. "Whatever. Are you sure you

erased everything? My dad will freak out if I get in any more trouble. He said the trustees are already having heart attacks over everything that's happened. As if any of it were *my* fault!"

Before I could answer, I heard footsteps. I turned, expecting Nigel again. Instead I saw Dr. Montgomery huffing and puffing as he pulled himself along with his cane.

"So this is where you ran off to," he panted at me. "What's all the commotion?"

"A TV reporter has been hanging around all day," I told him. "From one of the gossip shows. Name's Nigel Nabb. He was harassing Destiny by taking unauthorized footage of her."

Dr. Montgomery was Firth's biggest cheerleader. "Firth First" was practically his middle name. I was hoping that if he heard about Nigel, he might do something about him. The sooner the reporter left campus, the better.

But the former headmaster barely seemed to register that part of it. He was gazing at Destiny with a disapproving look in his pale, watery eyes.

"And what are you doing out in public in *that* getup, young lady?" he said sternly. "True, we don't have much experience with students of the female persuasion here at Firth. But I would expect any Firth student to show a bit more decorum than you're demonstrating at this particular moment. This is a public gymnasium, not your private boudoir."

Destiny just goggled at him for a moment. "But I—he was—," she sputtered. Then she threw both hands in the air. "Whatever!" She spun and stormed off through the locker room door.

Montgomery watched her go, tut-tutting softly to himself. Then he checked his watch.

"Oh, dear," he said. "I'm supposed to be home by now. I'd better be off or Mrs. Wilson will worry."

Mrs. Wilson was Dr. Montgomery's faithful longtime housekeeper. Everyone said the stout, stern woman had been at Firth almost as long as Montgomery himself. From what I'd seen since arriving on campus, he could do no wrong in her eyes, though she disapproved of just about everything and everyone else in the world. I doubted she'd hold it against him if he was a few minutes late.

"Listen, sir," I said. "About this Nigel Nabb guy—"

"That sounds like an issue for Dr. Darity to handle," Montgomery cut me off before I could finish. "Perhaps you should alert him to the problem. Good day, young man."

I shrugged as he hobbled off. "Oh well, I tried," I told Killer.

The dog barely spared me a glance. Whatever moment of teamwork we'd had seemed to have passed. With another shrug, I turned and headed for the exit myself.

When Killer and I got back to my cottage, Frank was waiting. "Glad you're here, bro," I told him, collapsing on the sofa. "I've had an interesting afternoon."

"Me too." Frank scratched Killer behind the ears as the dog pressed up against him like an eager puppy. "What'd you find out?"

We updated each other on our investigations. Frank looked thoughtful when he heard about Nigel's antics. And especially his comment about the campus troubles.

"Sounds like we need to add him to the suspect list," he said.

SUSPECT PROFILE

Name: Nigel Nabb

Hometown: Hollywood, California

Physical description: 5'11", 210 pounds, blond hair, gray-blue eyes, bad suits, lots of chest hair

"Sounds like our suspect list is getting pretty long again," I said as I watched him dash off an info request to HQ.

"So what else is new?" Frank countered with a wry smile. "Let's go over what we've got and see if we can narrow it down any."

I kicked up my feet on the coffee table. "Okay, so who've we got?" I said. "There's my new buddy Nigel Nabb, of course."

"Except that he just arrived on campus today. How could he have spiked the Winner's Cup yesterday, or messed with the soccer truck last week?"

"Maybe he *was* here and we just didn't know it," I said. "If the rumors are true about his show planting fake stories, he—or someone else from the show—could've sneaked up early and done that stuff."

"Just in time for the intrepid reporter to show up and film the scandalous aftermath," Frank finished. "Seems a little far-fetched. But I suppose it's possible. Who else have we got?"

"Destiny, Lee, maybe Darity or Spencer . . ."

"Don't forget Patton. Actually, I was wondering if he could be the one who called in Nigel."

I sat up. "What makes you wonder that?"

"I was thinking about that confrontation earlier today on the Green. Things were pretty tense, but when I looked over to see how Patton was reacting, he wasn't paying much attention. He was checking his watch and looking kind of distracted."

"Think he was waiting for Nigel to show?" I guessed. "Maybe because he knew he was coming?"

Frank shrugged. "Nigel *did* turn up just a minute or two after that."

"Interesting."

"Yeah. It could explain how Nigel could be

involved even though he wasn't even here when some of the stuff happened."

"Okay, sounds like a theory," I said. "But after what you found in those medical records, do you think we need to add your roomie to the mix too?"

"Zeke?" Frank looked uncertain. "It does seem odd that he's listed in there as an epileptic. I've been living with him for a couple of weeks now and had no idea."

"And he doesn't exactly seem like the secretive type." I smirked, recalling some of Zeke's antics. He was the type of guy who would think it was a blast to stroll into the dining hall totally naked just to get people to react. Probably the only thing holding him back was the cold.

"I'm not sure what his motive would be, though. And he seems way too lazy to hold a grudge and do anything about it." Frank looked thoughtful. "Anyway, much as I hate to say it, I'm thinking Lee is our best suspect right now."

After hearing about Lee taking that key, I had to agree. "Any idea what the key opens?" I asked.

"Nope. You've seen Darity's office—it's not exactly super organized."

I grinned. "Yeah. Aunt Trudy would faint if she saw it."

"Don't mention her name." Frank shuddered. "It reminds me how long it's taking to wrap things up here. And how much explaining we'll have to do when we get home."

"Let's not worry about that now," I said. "Let's focus on the mission."

"I guess you're right." Frank still looked anxious. What can I say? He was born to worry. "So what's our next step?"

I checked my watch. "There's still time before dinner. Let's take another look around for Lee."

We left Killer in his kennel and headed across campus toward the dorms. When we reached the Green, we heard a commotion.

"What now?" Frank muttered, glancing at a mob of students near the dining hall.

"One way to find out." I led the way over there.

A couple of dozen students were marching in a circle. Several were waving handmade signs. Most were chanting in unison. Something about broccoli.

"Broccoli?" I said, confused.

Frank pointed at the closest sign. "Check it out," he said. "Looks like they're protesting some new vegetarian menu in the cafeteria!"

oices of Dissent

"**V**egetarian menu?" Joe said. "Things are really getting tense around here if people are getting worked up about something like that."

I nodded, taking in another sign. This one read FIRTH FIRST, TOFU NEVER. I was distracted from that by hearing a kid I vaguely recognized from my history class shouting something about lentils being people too. A few students near him cheered.

Glancing over, I saw a counterprotest forming. It was a little smaller in numbers than the main protest, but its members looked just as irate.

Joe grabbed a passing protester. It happened to

be my roommate, Zeke. As usual, he was right in the thick of things.

"Dude," said Joe. "What's up with this? Why do you even care if they add veggie burgers to the caf?"

Zeke scowled. "It's not just about cafeteria food, man." He held up his sign, which read FIGHT THE POWER! in scrawled marker. "I heard this food thing is only the start. If Darity gets his way on that, he's planning to ban TV and Internet access in the dorms next. And who knows what after that. Slippery slope, man, slippery slope!"

"Hang on," I said, not really seeing the connection between tofu burgers and TV privileges. "Where are you getting all this? What makes you think Darity wants to do any of that stuff?"

Zeke shrugged. "FirthFirst, dude."

"What?"

"FirthFirst." Now he sounded impatient. He sounds like that a lot. Especially when he's talking to me.

Another protester heard him. "Yeah, that's where I saw it too," he said. He was an earnest-looking kid with curly hair. "This morning's post was all about it."

Joe blinked at Curly. "Post? What are you guys talking about?"

"Duh. The blog, dude!" Zeke said. "Check it out, maybe you'll get a clue."

He hurried off. That left us with Curly. "A blog?" I asked him. "What blog?"

"FirthFirst," the kid replied.

This was rapidly turning into a "Who's on First?" routine. But I thought I was starting to get the punchline. "You mean there's a blog called FirthFirst?" I guessed.

"Yeah. It's, like, an underground thing." Curly shot a look around. "Don't tell any teachers or whatever or it could get shut down."

I traded a look with Joe. Dr. Darity had bigger things on his mind than shutting down some student blog.

"So should we check it out?" Joe asked as Curly rushed off.

I glanced at my watch. "It'll have to wait until after dinner. We should get there early so we have plenty of time to talk to people."

"Like Lee," Joe guessed.

"And Patton, and maybe Spencer," I added. "Come on, let's head in."

Joe and I split up as we entered. As a school employee, he ate with the rest of the staff in a reserved section off to one side. I was in the main part of the dining hall with the students.

Most of the time I ended up eating with Spencer and the rest of the GTT crew. Today was no exception. I figured that should make it easy to question several of the people on our suspect list at once.

I thought about the case as I waited in the food line. Tonight was tuna casserole. Judging by the smell, we would've been better off with the tofu burgers.

When I emerged with my tray, Spencer and Lee were already at the usual table, along with Van and a few others. But someone else was missing.

"Where's Patton?" I asked as I sat down.

Spencer looked troubled. "Patton hasn't been sitting with us lately," he said.

"Yeah," Van put in with a snort. "Peachy banished himself."

"What do you mean?" I asked. "I noticed he wasn't sitting here at brunch, but I didn't think much about it."

That was true, though I didn't mention the reason for my lack of interest then. Namely, that we hadn't yet put him back on the suspect list.

Spencer sighed and rubbed his forehead. "It's really inside GTT business, Frank, but I know we can trust you not to spread it around," he said.

"See, we gave Patton the bad news yesterday. Officially, you know?"

"Let's just say he didn't take it too well," another senior brother said.

"Yeah." Spencer shook his head sadly. "Last year he took the news so well that we all hoped he'd do the same this time around. But this year it seems like he's way more bummed out about not making it in. Nobody from GTT told him he couldn't sit with us or hang out with us anymore. But he's pretty much gone into hiding as far as we're concerned."

One of the others glanced around the room. "Looks like he can't even stand to be in the same dining room with us," he said. "I don't see him anywhere."

"Nope, there he is," Lee said. "He's just a little late, that's all."

I followed his gaze. Patton had just entered the dining hall. He still looked a little overdressed, just as he had that morning. His wool coat was open to reveal a button-down shirt and dark slacks.

That made me flash back to my earlier conversation with Joe. Namely, the part where we'd speculated that Patton might have contacted Nigel Nabb. Could he be dressed up today because he knew he might end up on national TV?

As he emerged from the line with his tray a few

minutes later, Patton looked over at our table. But he turned away quickly, hurrying over to one nearby. It was empty except for three brothers named Albert, Aloysius, and Alastair, who were the primary members of a campus band called Devoured by Bears. The trio glanced at the newcomer only briefly before returning to their own conversation.

Interesting. It really did look as if Patton was holding a grudge.

And no wonder. Getting into GTT had seemed really important to him. And now he'd been denied not once, but twice. Could he be angry enough to lash out at the frat? If so, how did the stuff with Destiny figure in? Was it just because she was dating Lee? I hadn't thought many people knew about that, but you never knew. News *did* travel fast at Firth. . . .

I was distracted from my thoughts by a boisterous shout. It was Zeke. He was standing on the table, waving his protest sign.

That was nothing unusual. Zeke loved nothing more than being the center of attention. And he didn't much care how he got there.

The difference this time was that he actually had an interested audience. Nigel Nabb was standing there, filming away.

"That's it!" the reporter called out in his distinctive accent. "Tell me how you really feel, mate."

Uh-oh. Wandering around campus was one thing, but the dining hall seemed a lot more like private property. How had the reporter gotten in? I could only imagine what Dr. Darity and Dr. Montgomery would say when they caught Nigel stirring up trouble right under their noses.

I glanced toward the headmasters' table at the end of the room. Darity was nowhere in sight. But Dr. Montgomery was shooting an icy glare in Nigel's direction.

The GTT brothers were watching Zeke's antics too. "Man, I'm glad that clown never tried to rush," one of them muttered.

"Seriously," Van agreed. Seeing me watching Montgomery, he added, "I'm surprised old man Montgomery isn't stepping in to put a stop to the show."

"I'm surprised Darity hasn't kicked that Nabb dude off campus yet," another brother said. "He doesn't usually put up with that kind of mess."

Spencer glanced at Destiny, who was sitting at the next table. "Darity's had other things on his mind lately."

Lee grinned. "Whatever. Here comes Dr. M's enforcer. He'll probably send her over to knock some heads together."

I guessed he was referring to Mrs. Wilson, who had just hurried up to the headmasters' table. She shrugged off her coat and sat down in her usual seat beside Montgomery.

The two of them conferred briefly, their expressions grim. I was way too far away to hear them, but a moment later they both turned and stared at Nigel.

"Doesn't look like either of them is planning to do anything," I commented.

"You know how Dr. M is," Lee said, digging into his casserole. "Probably thinks it's not proper or whatever."

That made sense. Dr. Montgomery wore his strong sense of decorum and etiquette proudly and openly. The only thing that might stop him from kicking Nigel out himself was the fear that doing so might be seen as stepping on Dr. Darity's toes. So where *was* the headmaster, anyway?

"Yo, Frank!" Joe skidded to a stop beside the table, breathless and wide-eyed. "Did you hear? Someone totally trashed Darity's house!"

Damage Done

"**W**hoa!" I stared around me. "This is hardcore."

"Totally," Frank agreed. We were in Darity's house. The place looked like the mother of all tornados had torn through it. If tornados could write rude stuff on the walls in black spray paint, that is.

Every piece of furniture was tipped over or turned upside down. Shattered glass was everywhere, thanks to several broken windows, numerous cracked picture frames, and a bunch of smashed dishes. Clothes and bedding had been wadded up and stuffed in the toilets or trampled underfoot. Toothpaste and shampoo streaked the wallpaper, shaving cream dripped from the antique light fixtures, and food from the fridge was smeared all over everything. Toilet paper was looped up and down the staircase. Books were ripped and flung around. Every TV, stereo, and computer in the house lay smashed and broken on the floor.

We'd raced right over from the dining hall after I got the call. Darity had been waiting to hustle us inside.

"I can't believe it." The headmaster's voice shook a little as he looked around now. "Who would be sick enough to do something like this?"

"That's what we're going to find out, sir." Frank turned toward him. "I take it nobody was home when this happened?"

Darity pushed his glasses up his nose. "No," he said. "Destiny was at soccer practice, I suppose, and then dinner. And the housekeeper was in town doing some shopping. She's the one who discovered this—this mess, and called me on my cell."

"Where were you?" I asked.

"One of my meetings was canceled at the last minute, so I had a rare couple of free hours before dinner." The headmaster sighed, looking tired. "I decided to spend it taking a long walk in the woods to clear my mind. I was a little late getting back, so I was just heading straight to the dining hall when

Beatrice called. She was hysterical, as you can well imagine." His gaze wandered around the upstairs hallway, where we were standing at the moment. "I can't even fathom the level of anger that would cause someone to do this. As if they were determined to destroy absolutely everything in this house . . ."

I was still looking around. Frank and I have seen some vandalized places in our day. This one was pretty typical.

Or was it? Something was bugging me about what I was seeing. I just wasn't sure what it was.

"Hang on," I said as the answer finally clicked into place in my head. "I just noticed something."

"What?" Frank asked.

I moved down the hall, glancing into one room and then another. I wanted to be sure I was right before I said anything. Each look confirmed my idea.

"Check it out," I said. "The place looks like a wreck. But the damage is limited."

"What?" Darity stared at me as if I were crazy.

"No, seriously," I said. "Don't get me wrong, there's a ton of damage. But not to the house itself, really, or the antiques."

Frank got it right away. "Dr. Darity, is most of the furniture in here yours?" he asked. "I mean, your personal stuff that you brought with you when you moved in?"

"No," Darity replied. "The headmaster's residence comes furnished. Most of the furniture and rugs and such belong to the school."

Darity looked a little like an absentminded professor. But he was actually a pretty sharp guy. I could tell he was already catching on.

He hurried into a bedroom nearby. When we joined him, he was scanning the room.

"You're right," he said. "Most of my clothes and personal belongings—utterly destroyed. But that belongs to Firth." He pointed to an ancient-looking ceramic vase perched atop the fireplace mantel. You could have blown it over with a sneeze. But there it was, safe and sound despite the chaos all around it.

Frank glanced at the upended bedside table and a tipped-over chair. "The furniture looks like a mess, but nothing's really damaged, just tossed around," he said. "Once you have the rugs cleaned and the walls scrubbed, it'll all be good as new."

We headed back out to the hallway. "I guess this means I was the target here," Darity said grimly.

Frank nodded. "Looks that way. Whoever did this was sending a message either to you or to—"

"Oh, man!" Destiny Darity's voice yelled from

directly below us. "I thought those jerks at dinner were punking me. What happened?"

"Destiny!" Darity blanched. He leaned over the stair railing. "Don't come up here, sweetheart!"

Destiny ignored him, charging up the steps. "My room!" she shouted. "If they touched my stuff, I'll kill them!"

I winced, shooting Frank a look. We'd seen Destiny's room. Whoever had done this? He or she had *definitely* touched her stuff.

A moment later Destiny let out a wail. Yeah, she'd seen it too. She started ranting loudly about each damaged item.

"We should get her out of here," said Frank. "The police won't want her messing with the crime scene."

"Actually, I haven't called the police," Darity said. "I'd prefer to keep this incident quiet. Especially with that reporter fellow sniffing around. I haven't had a chance to track him down and escort him off campus yet, and if a story like this ends up in the national media, the trustees will have a fit."

Okay, so Darity was a busy guy. But hadn't he just said he'd taken a long walk in the woods? Seemed to me he might have used that time better. Like kicking Nigel's British behind out of Firth. But hey, what did I know?

"It might be too late to hush things up," Frank said. "It sounds like Destiny heard the news from someone at the dining hall."

"True." Darity looked troubled. "But surely nobody in the Firth community would share something like this with a reporter."

I wasn't so sure about that. But this was no time to argue about it.

"Okay." I glanced toward Destiny's room as a flurry of irritated curses floated out to us. "But cops or not, we still don't want her messing with the crime scene until *we* get a chance to look around."

"Gotcha," Darity said.

He led the way into Destiny's room. It was a mess, like the rest of the house. Then again, Destiny's room was always a mess. I wasn't sure how she could tell what the vandal had done.

She was still ranting and cursing angrily, flinging ripped and dirty clothes around. But just as we entered, she turned to face her bedside table. And suddenly went silent.

"Destiny?" her father said. "Come on, let's get you out of here, all right?"

Destiny didn't answer. When I looked at her, I did a double take. Were those . . . tears in her eyes? Even after everything that had happened to her, I'd never seen her cry before.

She picked up something from the bedside table. It looked like a photograph that had been ripped almost in half.

"Who would do this? Who could be so—so cruel?" she whispered. It was pretty clear she wasn't talking to us. Her eyes never left the photo.

I could see only part of it. The subject was a pretty, laughing woman with lush dark hair. She looked a lot like Destiny, actually. I guessed it had to be her late mother.

"Come on," Frank said softly. "Let's give her a minute."

I nodded and followed him out of the room. Darity stayed behind with his daughter.

"Okay, let's get started," said Frank.

He reached into his pocket and pulled out JuDGE. That's our nickname for our Junior Data Gathering Equipment device, courtesy of the geniuses at ATAC. One of JuDGE's coolest features is a tiny laser scanner beam. It's the latest technology. All you have to do is shine it on a surface, and it picks up any fingerprints that might be there.

We went to work. While Frank wielded the laser scanner, I took photos of everything with my ATAC-issue phone camera. I sent them to HQ as I went. The experts there could analyze them for any clues.

Good thing, too. Because Frank and I weren't turning up much. The only fingerprints we found belonged to Darity, Destiny, and the housekeeper.

"This is getting us exactly nowhere." Frank snapped the laser back into its spot in JuDGE's casing. "Maybe we should check out the entry point."

"Okay, where's that?" I said.

Frank shrugged. "I don't think Darity mentioned it. Let's go ask him."

It turned out Darity hadn't mentioned an entry point because there wasn't one. "There was no breaking and entering that I could find," he reported when we asked. "Either one of us forgot to lock up, or whoever did this had a key to get in."

Frank and I traded a look. I was sure he was thinking the same thing I was. That key he'd seen Lee take from Darity's office.

"Joe and I will double-check the possible entry points," Frank told Darity. "Maybe see if the access point could have been a broken window, or—what was that?"

I'd just heard what he'd heard. Shouts from somewhere outside.

We all rushed to the nearest window. Down below, by the front door, we saw Nigel peering through the viewfinder of his video camera. A lean, gray-haired woman was jumping around, yelling for him to stop.

"Uh-oh," Darity said grimly. "Looks like Beatrice needs some backup."

We all raced downstairs and outside. Nigel was still filming away. The housekeeper looked relieved to see us.

"I caught this scoundrel trying to peek in the windows," she cried.

"What's going on in there?" asked Nigel. "Looks mighty messy for a master's manse, eh?"

"This is private property," Darity said sternly. "If you don't leave right now, I'll have the police come and escort you off."

"And why's that, mate?" Nigel turned the camera on him. "Fancy Firth have something wicked to withhold?"

Just then he noticed me and Frank standing there. He blanched and looked around. I hid a smile as I realized what he was doing. Looking for Killer. For once, I wished I had old Fuzzy Face with me.

"Never mind, mates." Nigel shouldered his camera. "I've got all the footage I need for now. Night, all."

With that, he scurried away and disappeared

into the darkness. "Good riddance," Beatrice muttered.

"Hey!" Destiny appeared in the doorway behind us. She seemed to have recovered from her sadness. Now she just looked angry. She stomped up to her father, ignoring the rest of us. "I just found these in my room. Have you been snooping around in there?"

She held up a pair of wire-rimmed spectacles. Darity blinked at them in surprise.

"My reading glasses!" he said. "I've been looking everywhere for those. Lost them a couple of days ago."

"Was that while you were going through my stuff behind my back?" Destiny demanded.

Frank nudged me. "I think we've done just about all we can here," he murmured.

Back at my cottage, Frank and I talked over the latest.

"I keep thinking about that key," Frank mused from his position on the rug, where he was sitting rubbing Killer's ears. "But do you really think Lee could have done this?"

"Who knows?" I said. "He was at dinner, right?"

"Yeah. But you heard Darity. There was plenty

of time before that when anyone could've walked in and trashed his place."

"Anyone with a key," I corrected. "Unless someone left the door unlocked."

"We can't rule out that last possibility. People around here are pretty relaxed about locking up."

"Plus, Destiny would never win any responsibility contests," I added. "Okay, so where does that leave us with Lee?"

"Nowhere, I guess." Frank stood up and started pacing. Killer whined in disappointment, then started following him back and forth. "True, that could be why he snagged that key. But in an old house like that, it would be a pretty simple matter to pick the lock, too. Anyone could've done it."

"What about Destiny finding her dad's glasses in her room?" I said. "Think there's anything to that?"

Frank stopped pacing. "It could be just what she said. Maybe he was checking up on her and dropped them in there by accident. Or maybe the vandal found them somewhere else and tossed them there."

"Or what if Darity himself is the vandal?" I said. "We already know he doesn't have an alibi. And he knew the housekeeper would be out."

Frank nodded slowly. "It *would* be a good way to throw suspicion off himself."

I glanced at my laptop on the table nearby. "Hey, with all the excitement I almost forgot," I said. "We should check out that FirthFirst blog."

Frank was closer to the laptop. He grabbed it and logged on. It didn't take him long to find the blog. Soon it was loading.

I leaned over his shoulder for a look. My eyes widened as I saw what was on the home page.

There were photos of several people: Zeke, one of Firth's teachers, a couple of other students.

"All the people I found in those med records," Frank muttered. "The ones with epilepsy or similar seizure disorders."

"Yeah. And check this out," I said grimly, pointing to the banner headline above the photos. In huge red letters, it read SEIZE THE DAY!

Bad Sports

The next morning Zeke was gone before I woke up. For once. Usually the guy sleeps until, like, five minutes before his first class starts.

I wondered if he'd heard about the blog yet. If not, he was practically the only one. The whole campus was buzzing about it as I headed to my first class.

"Dude." Van fell into step beside me as I headed across the Green. "Did you see FirthFirst?"

"Yeah." I tried not to sound guilty. "I saw it."

Van shook his head. "Who knew all those people had epilepsy?" he said. "I mean, everyone knows about Charles. He's, like, totally open about it. So's what's-his-name from Allen House. But

Mr. Farley? And *Zeke*? Like, whoa! Who knew *they* were in the seizure squad?"

Apparently, nobody. Until now.

I couldn't help wondering if I was the reason for that. It seemed too coincidental that this kind of news would hit the blog less than twenty-four hours after I'd looked up the info on Darity's computer.

But no. I'd been careful to shut down the medical records site as soon as I was finished. And I hadn't breathed a word to anyone except Joe about what I'd found. The best we could figure was that Darity must have let word slip about that anticonvulsant drug being responsible for the Winner's Cup incident, and whoever was writing the blog had figured out the rest somehow.

But how? Those medical records were supposed to be top secret. No one except the headmaster and the medical staff had access to them.

When I arrived at English class, Mr. Westerley wasn't there yet. Most of the class was gathered around Patton's desk. He was perched on the edge of it, his acid-scarred face excited as he chattered about the latest gossip. Namely, that blog post.

"This just proves it," he was exclaiming as I came in. "Whoever's doing the blog knows *everything* that goes on around here. It's crazy!"

"Hey Peachy, you seem to know a lot about that blog," one of the guys said.

"Yeah," another put in. "And you're always ready to spread the word about it. Are *you* the FirthFirst blogger?"

Patton frowned. "I wish," he said. "I'm dying to know who's really behind the blog. It seems weird that it, like, came out of nowhere after all the bad stuff started this year." He waved a hand to indicate his own damaged face.

"Maybe it's Ellery," someone said. "He was always up to something, right? And he disappeared right around the time the blog got popular. Maybe he left school to join the blogosphere full time."

"That doesn't make sense," another kid put in. "How could Ellery keep up with all the gossip if he's not even at Firth anymore?"

I carefully kept my face neutral as I took my seat. Despite the way every little speck of gossip flew around this place, everyone still seemed clueless about Ellery's sudden departure. Chalk one up to the power of Mr. Marks's cover-up.

"Maybe Ell *is* still here." A GTT brother grinned. "He could be hiding out in the basement of Firth Hall. That place has so many nooks and crannies, nobody'd ever find him there."

Patton rolled his eyes. "Get real, you guys. Everyone knows Ellery left school to join the CIA as a junior spy. His dad's connected there, you know."

"Junior spy?" someone scoffed. "Grow up, Peachy. There's no such thing."

"Forget Ellery," someone else said. Slipping into a faux British accent, he added, "Oi think it's Noigel Nabb spreading all the gossip."

Most of the others laughed, and I smiled along. But I couldn't help wondering if the last guy was right. It did seem pretty coincidental that Nigel had appeared just when that blog was heating up.

Actually, there were a lot of coincidences lately. And I didn't like any of them. In my experience since joining ATAC, a coincidence was rarely just a coincidence. At least when it came to missions.

I was still pondering that as I hurried to my next class. Westerley had kept us a little late, so I had to jog to make it in before the late bell rang.

"So glad you could join us, Mr. Hardy," the teacher said wryly. He peered around the room. "You didn't bring Mr. Jenkins with you, did you?"

"Lee must be sick or something," one of my classmates offered. "He wasn't in trig just now either."

At that moment Lee himself rushed into the room. "Sorry I'm late," he exclaimed breathlessly. "I, uh, overslept."

The teacher started a rant about being prompt. But I wasn't listening. I was staring at Lee, feeling uneasy. Lee wasn't the type to oversleep.

So what was up with him now? Had he lost track of time while sneaking around with Destiny? It seemed possible. Destiny herself wasn't known for promptness or following the rules. Maybe her bad influence was rubbing off on Lee.

But I also kept thinking back to that stolen key. I hated to think that Lee was the person we were after. But it was hard to ignore what I'd seen. Until we found out what that key was for, we had to keep him at the top of our list.

After classes finished for the day, I decided to pay a visit to Firth's soccer coach. One of the incidents that neither Ellery nor Casey had confessed to was the way the swim coach had been injured in the soccer office. Joe and I had questioned both coaches about the incident earlier in the mission, but I figured it couldn't hurt to revisit the issue. There had to be some connection we were missing; something to tie all the incidents together. We just had to find it.

When I reached the office, the coach was nowhere in sight. But someone else had clearly been there just before me. Written on the office door in bright red liquid was a message:

"Whoa," I breathed as I took it in. The pungent, distinctive smell told me what the red liquid was. Blood.

I quickly pulled out my cell phone and snapped a couple of pictures. Then I carefully touched one finger to the blood. Still wet.

I shot a look around. Whoever had left this message couldn't have gone far.

CREAK!

I spun around. That noise had come from right behind me! I was just in time to catch the briefest glimpse of a foot disappearing around the corner.

"Stop!" I yelled, taking off after the person. "Who are you?"

There was no answer except the clatter of footsteps. I raced after them, rounding the corner into a hallway just in time to hear the steps fading away around the next bend.

I chased the sound. Bursting through a doorway, I found myself in a small workout room full of free weights and other gym equipment. I stopped, scanning the room. At first I didn't see anything.

Then a flash of movement caught my eye at one end. I spun around... just in time to see a whole net full of medicine balls come loose, sending a dozen weighted balls bouncing toward me!

"Hey!" I yelped, raising both hands to fend off the heavy balls.

By the time I fought my way through the Attack of the Medicine Balls, I could hear a few thumps off in the next hallway. I ran that way. But my path was blocked by a pile of mats that had been shoved across the hallway!

Running footsteps taunted me from the far side of the jumbled pile of mats. I clambered over the mats as quickly as I could. But by the time I reached the far side, there was no sign of my quarry. However, I did see a door nearby flapping as if someone had just rushed through it.

The door led directly outside. I emerged into the bright afternoon sunshine and found myself in the middle of a huge crowd. People were milling around everywhere, some of them holding signs.

I groaned and collapsed back against the wall to catch my breath. Great. Another protest. And my quarry had already blended in with the crowd. Maybe if I'd had Killer with me, he could have tracked the person down.

But on my own, it was pretty much hopeless.

On the Run

"Hey." I tugged on Killer's leash. "This is supposed to be your midmorning exercise walk, not a Dumpster dive. Trust me, if you're not into it, I've got better things to do."

Killer whined and pulled even harder toward the huge metal trash container behind the cafeteria. I gave another tug, my annoyance building. With time ticking away and Frank and me no closer to wrapping up our mission, the last thing I needed right now was doggie problems. As it was, Killer's detailed schedule was definitely cramping my ATAC style.

"I thought well-trained law-enforcement machines like you didn't care about stinky kitchen scraps from the caf," I said as Killer gave the leash another yank. "Guess you're just a dog after all."

He ignored me. What else was new?

Normally I wouldn't think twice about a dog being interested in a giant trash bin. Especially one with the aromatic scents of that morning's bacon and pancakes wafting out of it.

But it really wasn't Killer's usual style. Then again, I wouldn't put it past him to develop new bad habits just to make me look bad. Yeah, he liked me *that* much.

"Dude, come on!" I insisted, pulling harder to try to get Killer moving.

But the dog planted his fuzzy little paws. It's amazing how hard it is to drag a hundred-pound dog that doesn't want to be dragged. Pricking his ears forward, Killer let out several loud, sharp barks.

I opened my mouth to yell at him. But just then I heard the clatter of cans and cardboard boxes falling over. A second later a figure darted out from behind the Dumpster and took off.

"Hey!" I blurted out. "Stop!"

Going on instinct, I took off after the figure. A dark hoodie covered the person's head and torso, making it impossible to tell whether it was male or female, black or white, old or young—though I didn't know of any Firth students quite that small and slender. Maybe an extra-petite female member of the school staff?

I scanned my mind for likely candidates but couldn't come up with anyone except Ida from the mailroom, who was about two hundred years old and probably didn't even know what a hoodie was. There weren't really that many females on campus. It definitely wasn't Destiny—way too short.

Killer was racing along in front of me, pulling at the leash and barking fiercely. "Shut up, Killer!" I shouted. "Listen, whoever you are—you don't have to be scared of the dog. He just wants you to stop, okay?"

The only response from Runaway Hoodie was to speed up and dash around the corner of the cafeteria building. Okay, so maybe he or she wasn't afraid of Killer. In which case, I *really* wanted to know why he or she was running away.

Killer and I took the corner at a dead run. The dog was faster than me and proved it, almost scraping me against the edge of the brick wall as he whipped around after our quarry.

"Oh, man," I muttered, wincing at the road rash on my elbow. Or should that be wall rash? In any case, I was glad I had the dog with me. He'd already proved his tracking abilities. Even if Hoodie McHooderson could outrun me, he or she couldn't outrun Killer's finely honed nose.

Our quarry led us on a merry chase around the cafeteria building and down another alleyway. I still hadn't gotten a good look at him/her/it. But Killer and I were definitely closing ground. One more jump . . .

I burst out from the alleyway just a dozen feet behind my quarry. But then Killer stopped so quickly that I almost tripped over him.

"Whoa!" I yelped, catching myself on his furry neck before I did an embarrassing—and probably painful—somersault over his back.

Then I saw why he'd stopped. Nigel Nabb was standing right in front of us, camera in hand. The dog stared at him and let out a warning growl.

"There, there, pretty puppy," said Nigel, sounding a little nervous. "Sorry we got off on the wrong paw during our last encounter. I didn't realize then that you were the marvelous mascot I'd heard so much about."

"What are you doing here?" I demanded, more than a little annoyed by the interruption. A quick glance ahead showed no sign of that hoodied figure. "I thought Darity told you to get off campus last night."

"Another day, a fresh start," Nigel said blithely.

He peered into my face. "Funny how I keep running into you everywhere, mate. What's your name? And where were you and the pooch off to in such a hurry, eh?"

"Does Dr. Darity know you're back?" I asked.

I was pretty sure I knew the answer. If I'd had any doubts, Nigel's smirk answered them.

"I don't need permission to report the news," he said.

"News? Is that what you call the idiotic gossip you report about?"

"Ah, so you're a fan of the show?" Nigel's smirk grew. "Then you'll know that I never give up on a story. Now, would you care to answer my questions, mate?"

"Nope." I gave a tug on Killer's leash. "Come on, boy."

Killer obeyed. For once. Maybe that meant he liked Nigel even less than he liked me. Yay me.

Nigel shrugged and wandered off. That was kind of a relief. For a second there I'd been afraid he was onto me. Nope. He was just being obnoxious.

I thought about trying to have Killer track that person in the hoodie. But I wasn't sure it was worth it. Thanks to Nigel, Hoodie now had a pretty good head start. Enough to shake us by walking through water or any of the other usual tricks.

"Come on, boy," I said with a sigh. "Let's go home."

We were on the winding, pine-lined path leading toward the staff cottages when Killer pricked his ears forward. I followed his gaze and saw someone creeping along just ahead, moving slowly and peering carefully around with each step.

It was dim in the shade of the trees, so I couldn't tell if it was the same person I'd just been chasing. He or she disappeared around a curve in the path. I shot forward.

"Aha!" I cried, rounding the corner and grabbing the figure by the arm. "Gotcha!"

"Oh!" someone shrieked.

The figure spun around, looking guilty and a little frightened. It was a slim, attractive young woman with auburn hair. I didn't recognize her. And trust me, I have an excellent memory for attractive young women.

"Who are you?" I asked.

She shook off my grip on her arm. "I should ask you the same question," she said, her voice shaking a little. "Touch me again and I'll scream!"

"Hey, what's wrong? I heard you scream. . . ." Another young woman hurried into view from ahead.

This one I recognized. "Janice?" I said.

"Joe?" Janice was one of my fellow Firth staff members. I sat with her and some other pals for most meals. Her eyes flicked from me to the other woman and back again. "What's going on?"

I glanced at Killer. He was sitting there calmly, not seeming too interested in any of this. Great. Some help he was.

"You know this creep, Jan?" the other woman exclaimed. "He ran up behind me and grabbed me!"

"There must be some misunderstanding," Janice said soothingly. "This is just Joe. He's Killer's new handler. Joe, this is Mary. She used to work here."

"Oh." I was starting to realize that this was one big misunderstanding. For one thing, Mary was definitely taller than the hooded figure from earlier. "Um, sorry about that. I thought you were someone else. Why were you sneaking along like that?"

Mary traded a look with Janice. For a second I thought they weren't going to answer. But finally Janice did.

"Mary is Mrs. Wilson's niece," she said. "She lives down in Sugarview."

Dr. Montgomery's housekeeper wasn't very popular with the rest of the staff. Actually, that was an understatement. Mrs. Wilson was a favorite topic of gossip among Janice and her friends.

They thought she was stuck-up because she kept to herself and didn't socialize with the other employees. I also vaguely recalled some talk of a niece who lived in the nearby town of Sugarview. One who didn't like her aunt any more than the others did.

"I was just visiting some friends," Mary spoke up, looking kind of sheepish by now. "I was sneaking because I didn't want you-know-who to see me." She waved a hand in the general direction of the Cottage, which was fairly close by. "My aunt and I don't get along too well."

Janice nodded. "That insufferable woman's superior attitude chased Mary right out of Firth," she said. "You'd think Mrs. Wilson was a member of Dr. M's stupid secret society herself the way she acts!"

I perked up at that. "Are you talking about the Brothers of Erebus?" I asked, doing my best to sound casual. "Um, I think I heard something about that."

Janice shrugged. "I guess that's what it's called."

"Yeah." Mary rolled her eyes. "But Aunt Myrna practically bit my head off the one time I tried to ask her about it. Only thing I know for sure is she thinks it makes her hot stuff just 'cause she works for a member."

"Stupid if you ask me," Janice muttered.

"Anyway, I was hoping when the new head-master took over he might kick my aunt out of Firth," Mary went on. "But no luck so far."

"Too bad," Janice put in. "Then you could come back and work here again!"

Her friend smiled. "I know, wouldn't that be awesome? But it's not looking good. Dr. Darity doesn't seem to care if she stays. And I know that old witch will never leave Firth on her own. Not so long as Dr. Montgomery is around."

"Or maybe longer." Janice grimaced. "They're two of a kind, those two. Neither of 'em believes in change."

"Okay," I said. "But listen, about the Brothers of Erebus . . ."

I questioned them a little more. But it soon became clear that neither knew any more about the secret society. I should have known better than to get my hopes up. Nothing on this mission was that easy.

"And . . . send," I mumbled to myself, hitting a button on the laptop. I'd just written up the latest developments for HQ. Not that there was much to report.

After dinner, Frank and I had met to go over

the mission. It wasn't much of a meeting, though. Neither of us had any new theories or much new information.

We'd also called Darity to check in. He'd found out that some of that anticonvulsant med was indeed missing from the school infirmary.

That was good to know. But it didn't really tell us much.

Feeling frustrated, I clicked over to the Firth-First blog. I'd been checking it whenever I got the chance. There hadn't been a new entry since the epilepsy thing last night.

Until now. I gasped as I saw my brother's photo pop up on the screen. WHO IS THIS "STUDENT"? the caption read. AND WHAT IS HE *REALLY* DOING AT FIRTH? FULL "REPORT" COMING SOON. . . .

Out of Place

I awoke to someone choking me. "Hey!" I sputtered, shoving at the hands wrapped around my neck. They didn't let go.

Acting on ATAC-schooled instinct, I dug my fingernails into my attacker's hands. At the same time I brought up both legs and kicked out as hard as I could.

"Oof!"

My eyes flew open. I sat up and saw Zeke sprawled on the floor by my bed. He was rubbing his stomach. Guess that's where my feet connected.

"Dude!" he complained. "Where'd the kung fu moves come from?"

"Are you nuts? What were you doing?" I swung my feet over the edge of my bed.

He scowled. "I should ask you the same thing," he snapped. "I always knew there was something shady about you, man! Turning up in the middle of the semester like that, stealing my sweet single room . . ."

I blinked the rest of the sleep out of my eyes. He looked angry. No, outraged. That was weird. Usually Zeke was too lazy to bother with such strong emotions.

"What's wrong?" I asked. "Are you mad about something?"

"Duh!" He rolled his eyes. "It was you, wasn't it? Tell the truth!"

"It was me what?"

"Everyone knows now. It was on the blog."

This was starting to get annoying. "*What* was on the blog?" I demanded. "You're not making any sense, Zeke."

"I just got a text from a buddy." Zeke glared at me, looking sullen. "Said you're the one who leaked those med records."

"What?"

"Yeah. Said he saw on FirthFirst that you're working with that Nigel dude. You know—the TV guy."

"I know who he is." I rubbed my eyes, trying

to make sense of this. "But your friend is wrong. I never met Nigel before this weekend. Why would anyone think I'm working with him? That's crazy."

Zeke shrugged. "Dunno. The blog got taken down, I guess. But it said you're an imposter or something. And that means it had to be you who spilled the stuff about my seizure disorder." His scowl grew deeper. "The last thing I want is to be lumped in with all those freaks who, like, have grand mals all the time and stuff. I just got diagnosed with a super-mild case as a kid. Haven't had an attack or even taken any meds in, like, years." He shrugged. "It's only even in the school records because my mom's a freak with the worrying. She's afraid I could have a relapse or something."

Okay. At least part of this was starting to make sense. A little, anyway. Zeke thought I was the one who'd told everyone about his condition, so he'd jumped on me in a fit of temper. Pretty typical for him, really.

I realized it also meant that Zeke probably wasn't our culprit. If he was telling the truth about his disorder, he wouldn't have access to that medication after all. I made a mental note to double-check what he'd said. But I was pretty much convinced that he was out as a suspect. He'd never been much of one anyway.

"Look, I'm sorry you're upset or whatever," I told him. "But I didn't have anything to do with spilling your secrets."

I only hoped that was true. It still seemed weird that the blog post had popped up right after I'd accessed those medical records.

But at the moment I was more worried about the rest of what Zeke had said. What was this business about me being on the blog? Zeke didn't seem to know any more than he'd already told me.

I checked my watch to see if there was time for a stop at Joe's cottage. But no such luck. I'd have to book it if I even wanted to make it to class on time. Everything else would have to wait.

"Where's Lee?" a kid named Phil asked as the late bell rang to start second period.

The teacher heard him and looked up with a frown. "Excellent question, young man," he said. "Mr. Jenkins has been late more than once lately."

The door flew open and Lee rushed in. "I'm here, sorry!" he cried breathlessly. He almost dropped his books as he hurried toward his seat. "Honestly, I'm really sorry, sir. Won't happen again."

"But it *has* happened again. And again." The

teacher peered at him sternly over his bifocals. "And I must remind you, Mr. Jenkins. You didn't exactly set the world on fire with your last quiz grade."

A few of the other students snickered loudly. "Goes to show a charity case can't hack it at Firth," someone whispered loudly.

I wasn't sure whether the teacher heard the comment or not. But Lee definitely had. I saw his face blanch. He didn't respond, though. Just ducked his head and took his seat.

When the bell rang to send us to third period, I was still thinking about Lee. He was in my next class, too. Phys ed. The teacher, Mr. Larch, was pretty tough. He usually worked us hard on the equipment in the high-tech workout room. But if I grabbed a machine next to Lee, maybe I'd have the opportunity to chat with him.

What would I say? I wasn't sure. I hated to think that Lee could really be the one we were after. ATAC had taught us never to assume anything. Still, it was hard to imagine that someone like Lee could be capable of some of the stunts we were talking about. Like trying to run down his own girlfriend with that soccer truck. Or trashing Darity's house.

But the evidence was starting to pile up against

him. His sudden rash of tardiness. Seeing him steal that key. The mysterious thumps inside his room when he'd refused to answer the door.

When I walked into the gym, I scanned it for Lee. I spotted him over near the pommel horse. I also spotted someone else.

"What's Dr. Montgomery doing here?" I asked the kid next to me.

He shrugged. "Must be our sub," he said. "I heard Larch is out with the flu or something."

Dr. Montgomery was leaning on his cane at the far end of the gym. As usual, he was impeccably dressed. Three-piece suit. Matching tie and hand-kerchief. Shiny shoes. The whole deal. He looked as out of place in the smelly gym as a sweaty weight lifter would in the U.S. Senate.

I walked over to Lee. "Hey," I greeted him. "So is Montgomery really our substitute today?"

Lee shrugged. "Guess so. He does step in a lot for the other teachers. But this is the first time I've ever heard of him subbing for gym class."

Most of the class was there by now. Dr. Mont-gomery hobbled to the center of the gym. I winced as I saw his cane slide a bit on the slick floor. But he made it in one piece.

"Greetings, gentlemen," he said in his quaver-ing voice. "I would say 'gentlemen and lady,' but we seem to be missing the lady in that equation. Does anyone know where Miss Darity might be?"

"Late as usual, probably," someone called out. A few others laughed.

Dr. Montgomery didn't look amused. "Well, perhaps she'll turn up soon. In any case, as I'm sure you've deduced by now, I shall be stepping in for Mr. Larch today." His face stretched into a rueful half smile. "I'm sure some of you are thinking that the gymnasium isn't quite my usual milieu. . . ."

There was some more laughter at that. Montgomery chuckled along.

"However, the show must go on," he said. "We'll make the best of it if we all pull together. Firth First!"

"Firth First!" someone called back, while a couple of others whooped.

I was relieved. With Montgomery in charge, it should be easier to find some time to talk to Lee.

A few of the guys were already drifting toward the door leading to the exercise room. But Dr. Montgomery stopped them.

"We'll be trying something different today," he announced. "I realize you're all accustomed to working out on the fancy modern gym equipment that some of our alumni have been generous enough to provide. However, there is value in more old-fashioned Firth-style exercise as well. I'm going to show you that right now."

"Oh, man," someone near me grumbled. "Typical Dr. M. Why do anything normal when you can pretend you're living in some past century?"

Lee grinned. "It'll be cool. Dr. M is just an old-fashioned guy at heart, that's all."

The former headmaster was already directing several of the students to pull out some equipment from the big closets along one wall. Soon they were hauling around a bunch of exercise mats and medicine balls.

"I'll be dividing you into teams or two or three," said Dr. Montgomery. "Then you shall rotate among different stations, performing various exercises."

He went on to describe those exercises. Push-ups on the mats. Tossing the heavy medicine balls back and forth. Climbing the rope dangling from the ceiling in one corner of the gym. Jumping rope. Doing chin-ups. That kind of stuff.

I was ready to volunteer to be Lee's partner. That way we should definitely have a chance to talk. But Dr. Montgomery beat me to the punch.

"Mr. Hardy, Mr. Jenkins, you two will be team one," he said. "Miss Darity can join you if she deigns to show up." There was a glimmer of disapproval in his eyes when he mentioned Destiny. She might get away with being tardy in some of her classes. But I guessed Dr. Montgomery wasn't the type to let it slide.

He went on to name the other teams. I glanced at Lee. "Guess this could be kind of fun," I said.

"Sure. I'm always up for something different."

After he finished dividing up the class, Montgomery assigned each team to its first station. Lee and I ended up with the rope climbing.

We headed over there. My mind was already back on the mission.

"So I hope Destiny's okay," I said, trying to sound casual. "You heard what happened to her house, right?"

I wasn't worried about telling secrets there. Even though Darity hadn't called the police, the entire campus knew about the vandalism. Typical Firth.

Lee shot a look at Montgomery. "Yeah. She's okay," he said, sounding distracted. "Destiny's pretty tough."

"I know. But it can't be easy. Especially after everything that's happened lately."

We were at the rope by now. Lee glanced up it.

"We should probably get climbing," he said. "I don't want to get in trouble if Montgomery thinks we're goofing off. He may look mild mannered, but he's a pretty strict discipline guy."

He sounded kind of nervous. Was he worried that all those tardies were starting to add up?

"Okay," I said. "I'll go first if you want."

There was a big stack of mats near the rope. Someone had tossed a couple right underneath it. Lee and I kicked them into place, then I grabbed the rope.

"Go for it, bro," he said. "I'll spot you."

I nodded and started to climb. Hand over hand, up and up. Six feet, twelve . . . My mind wasn't really on the exercise. I was back to thinking about the mission. If Lee and I finished our climbs quickly, maybe he'd be more willing to talk while we waited for our next rotation. . . .

"Frank!" Lee's voice drifted up to me, sounding worried. "Hey, man. It looks like the rope is . . ."

I didn't hear the rest. That's because I'd just felt the rope sort of jerk in my hands. I gasped, tightening my grip.

But it was no use. The rope jerked again.

Then it came loose somewhere above me. I was falling, the floor rushing up at me.

Surprising Discoveries

"Frank!" I burst into the infirmary, breathing hard after sprinting halfway across campus. "Dude, you're okay!"

Frank was sitting up on one of the cots. He looked totally normal.

"Ah, you must be the cousin." The school nurse, an efficient woman named Ms. Randall, bustled over. "Frank was very lucky. Very lucky indeed."

"Yeah." Frank grinned at me. "Good thing I know how to fall. And that there was a big pile of mats nearby to fall onto."

I collapsed against the wall. I'd just returned from one of Killer's walks when Ms. Randall had called to tell me Frank had fallen off some high rope in the gym. She'd called it an accident. But I had my doubts. After tossing the dog into his kennel, I'd hightailed it over.

"Excuse me!" a whiny female voice broke in from behind a curtain nearby. "I asked for a glass of water, like, an hour ago."

"Destiny," Frank murmured as I moved closer. "She was here when I got here. Food poisoning. Or so she claims."

"I'm coming, Miss Darity." Ms. Randall sounded annoyed. "But it wasn't an hour ago. It was less than five minutes. And you're not my only patient, young lady."

Frank looked amused. "Based on my amazing investigative skills, it sounds like this isn't the first time she's used that excuse to get out of gym class," he whispered.

"Big surprise there," I said. "But listen, are you sure you're okay? What happened?"

Frank looked at the nurse. "Let's see if we can bust me out of here so we can talk."

It took some convincing. But Frank is good at sweet-talking adults. Finally he convinced Ms. Randall that he was okay and got himself released.

Once we were outside, he told me what had happened with the rope. "We should try to get a look at it to see if it looks like it was cut on purpose," he said. "But we shouldn't rule out the idea that this one was a genuine accident. After all, who could have predicted that old Dr. M would decide to make it old-school gymnasium day?"

"Good point. Unless someone knew he'd be subbing for Mr. Larch today and took advantage?"

"I suppose it's possible." Frank shrugged. "Anyway, that's not all we need to talk about. . . ."

He went on to fill me in about what had happened with Zeke. That reminded me to tell him about the blog post I'd seen last night.

"I contacted HQ right away," I told him. "One of the computer whizzes there hacked in and deleted it. But I guess a few people saw it before that."

"Yeah." Frank shook his head ruefully. "Like Zeke's buddy, for one. I'm afraid our cover might be blown for good this time."

"Not really," I argued. "There wasn't any mention of ATAC at all. People obviously think the quotes around 'report' mean you're with *R and F Report.*"

"I know. But even if people think I'm connected with Nigel, it's going to make it tough to get info out of them." He checked his watch. "Whoa, it's late. I need to get to class."

I rolled my eyes. "Are you kidding? You just said it yourself. Our cover is pretty much blown.

So who cares if you're late to class? Do you really want to let your obsessive nerdiness be the reason for our first failed mission ever?"

He frowned. "Well, what do you suggest?"

"How about doing everything we can to solve this thing before ATAC pulls us out?"

"But most of our suspects are going to be in class for the next few hours."

"Exactly." I smiled. "That makes it the perfect time to snoop around the dorms."

Even Frank couldn't argue with that. We didn't waste any time getting started.

We began at the GTT house. Spencer's room was neat as a pin, as always. That made it easy to figure out that nothing was out of place there.

"No big surprise," Frank said as he logged off of Spencer's laptop and set it carefully back in place. "He's always been a weak suspect at best."

We headed for Lee's dorm next. This time his door wasn't locked. We tiptoed in and took a look around. It looked like your typical dorm room. Dirty socks on the floor. Books everywhere. Celtics posters and pictures of cute girls on the wall.

"I don't see anything suspicious here," said Frank. "And it looks like he has his laptop with him. At least it's not here."

I'd just leaned down to peek under the bed.

"Hang on," I said. "Check this out. He's got, like, a whole trash dump down here."

"What do you mean?" Frank kneeled down to look for himself. The space beneath the bed was crammed with soda cans, bags from burger joints, and junk food wrappers of all kinds. A lot of them. As in, a *lot*.

I pulled out a candy bar wrapper. "Looks like Lee has a real junk food fixation."

"But why would he keep the wrappers under here?" Frank looked puzzled. "As far as I know, there are no rules about junk food at Firth, or eating in the dorms, or anything like that. Why wouldn't he just toss this stuff?"

"And how does he eat this much junk and not weigh three hundred pounds?" I shrugged. "Maybe he's got an eating disorder or something."

"That would explain the secrecy, I guess." Frank looked dubious. "Anyway, let's keep going. I want to see if we turn up that key he took."

We continued our search. I checked the bookcases and closet while Frank took on Lee's messy desk. After a moment I heard him make the funny little "hmm" noise he always does when he's found something interesting.

"What is it?" I asked.

Frank glanced up at me. "This is a little weird.

I just found a pamphlet with the bus routes and fares between Sugarview and Boston."

"What's so weird about that? Lee's from Boston, remember?"

"That's not the weird part." Frank held up something that looked like a computer printout. "There's also a reservation slip for a ticket to Boston. For late tomorrow night."

I blinked. "Tomorrow? Why would he go down there in the middle of the school week?"

"And in the middle of the night." Frank looked troubled. "Think he might be planning to run away from Firth for some reason?"

We couldn't come up with any good answers for that. So we kept searching. But we never did find any sign of that key.

Finally we gave up and moved on to Patton's room. "Do you really think Peachy could be our guy?" I wondered as I poked around a stack of magazines and other papers on his bedside table. "He's not exactly the master criminal type."

"I know. It'll be kind of embarrassing if it turns out he's outwitted us all this time." Frank finished flipping through the clothes in the closet and wandered toward me. "But he does have a pretty good motive to cause trouble. Getting into GTT seemed really important to him."

There was a printed program in the stack I was going through. It was from a chamber concert at a church hall down in Sugarview. "Wow, who knew Peachy was so cultured?" I commented. I was about to toss the program aside when Frank grabbed it out of my hand.

"Hey," he said. "Looks like this concert was this past Sunday afternoon."

"So what?" I was already moving on to the pile of school papers on Patton's desk.

"So that's why Patton was so dressed up that day."

I glanced at him with a smirk. "Did you catch the fashion bug from all the preppy boys here, bro?"

"No, I'm serious." Frank stared at the program. "This means Patton was off campus all afternoon. Probably from soon after Nigel's arrival to when we saw him come in for dinner. He didn't even have time to change clothes."

I'd just come to Patton's last chemistry test. There was a big red D scrawled in the corner, along with a note from the teacher warning that if Patton didn't catch on soon, he was going to blow himself up.

"I think I just found the evidence that it was Peachy who blew up the GTT tree the other day," I joked.

Frank glanced over at the test. "Actually, I think we just proved the opposite," he said, pointing again to that concert program.

"Huh?"

"If Patton was at this concert on Sunday afternoon, it means he wasn't on campus when that bomb went off," said Frank. "Have you seen a calendar anywhere?"

"Right here." I grabbed Patton's weekly planner off his desk and flipped back to the previous weekend. There was a notation on Sunday: *Concert with Great-Aunt R.*

"That doesn't necessarily prove he didn't do it," I pointed out. "He could've set the bomb on a timer or something. And then made sure he was off campus so he wouldn't be suspected."

"True. *If* he was capable of making a bomb like that in the first place." Frank waved a hand at the chemistry test. "That seems to indicate he doesn't have the know-how to pull it off."

A couple of quick phone calls, and we were both convinced. Patton had been nowhere near Firth for most of Sunday; the school's limo driver had dropped him off in Sugarview and picked him up later. And Patton's science teacher confirmed that he barely knew a compound from a test tube. That seemed to rule him out as our bomb maker.

"Okay, so Patton's off the hook for that," Frank said. "Do we still think he could be behind the other stuff?"

"Not really. Except maybe changing Lee's grades. That could've been totally unconnected to the rest, though. Just Peachy messing with the guy he saw as his main competition."

"So Patton is out. Spencer is probably out unless something new turns up." Frank shrugged. "Who else have we got?"

"Nigel Nabb. Lee. Maybe Darity."

"Or Destiny," Frank added. "Although I doubt she has the discipline to pull off most of this stuff and then keep quiet about it."

I nodded and checked my watch. "Come on, we'd better get out of here," I said. "Classes will be letting out soon. Let's lie low at my place and figure out what to do next."

"Are you sure we shouldn't take Killer with us?" Frank asked as he watched me close the dog's kennel door behind him. "He'd be a handy excuse if we get caught."

"We won't get caught." I clicked the kennel door shut and tested it. "Besides, who's going to believe we just happened to be walking the dog in Darity's office? After dark?"

Frank grinned. "Guess you're right. Come on, let's go."

Soon we were heading into Firth Hall, It was almost nine o'clock, and we expected the place to be empty and dark. Frank was pretty sure he could get access to the headmaster's computer again, plus we wanted to see whether that key was back in its spot.

But we got an unpleasant surprise. The lights were all on, and Darity was there despite the late hour. His office door was ajar, and we could see him sitting inside with several serious-looking men.

". . . and while we appreciate your passion for progress, Dr. Darity, we're concerned that you're changing too much, too fast," one man was saying.

Another joined in. "Yes. Firth has always been a place with strong traditions," he said. "We fear your, er, *improvements* may be the reason for all the recent unpleasantness."

"Indeed," the first man put in. "Dr. Montgomery would never say so directly, of course, but I've known him long enough to see that he's worried about the way things have been going these past few years as well."

"I understand your concerns, gentlemen," Dr. Darity spoke up, his voice somber and controlled.

"But I assure you, I have only the best for Firth in mind."

"But surely you can see our concerns," one of the men said. "It's one thing to bring the school into the computer age. But doing away with long-cherished traditions? Changing the very makeup of the student body? Those are harder for some of us to swallow."

"Are you referring to my daughter?" Darity asked. "Because she's a one-time exception. I have no intention of making Firth coed."

"That's all very well and good," the first man said. "But she is not our only concern, or indeed, even the greatest. . . ."

Frank shot me a look. "Sounds like those must be the trustees, or maybe some of the important alums," he whispered.

"We'd better scoot," I murmured. "Don't want to get caught eavesdropping."

We moved off far enough to talk normally. "So now what?" Frank said with a frown.

"It sounded like they were just getting started in there," I said. "Darity might be in for a long night."

Frank sighed. "Okay, time for plan B. Let's grab Killer and see if he can sniff out anything around any of the crime scenes."

It seemed like kind of a weak plan. But I couldn't come up with a better one, so I agreed.

We headed back to my cottage. When we got there, the first thing I saw was Killer's kennel door standing open.

"Oh, man," I muttered. "That stupid mutt must have busted out! I just hope he didn't go far."

"Hey." Frank sounded worried. I turned to see him hurrying toward the cottage's front door. It, too, was standing open.

I jogged after him. When I got inside, he was staring at an open cupboard. The one where Killer's food was kept. Then he glanced at the hook where his leash normally hung. Empty.

"Check it out," he said, sounding grim. "Unless Killer is smart enough to pack a bag, looks like he didn't leave on his own."

Dog Gone

It was a good thing I probably wouldn't be at Firth for much longer one way or another. Because I didn't hear a word Mr. Westerley said in English class the next morning.

Killer was still missing. So far, though, Joe and I were the only ones who knew that. Aside from whoever had dognapped him, of course.

The fact that the dognapper had taken Killer's leash and dog food gave us hope that he was okay. But that didn't stop us from worrying. A trained ex-police dog like Killer wasn't likely to prance off with just anyone like some overfriendly pet golden retriever. Who could have taken him? And how?

I couldn't help recalling that meeting we'd overheard in Darity's office. Was Killer one of those dusty old Firth traditions that the new headmaster would prefer to see go away?

Or could Nigel be behind this? He might be killing two birds with one stone. Getting back at Killer (and Joe) for scaring him by the pool, while also creating a better story for his show. After all, people were suckers for tales of animals in peril.

Joe was killing two birds with one stone that day too. He'd headed down to Sugarview right after breakfast. That way he got himself out of sight for a while so people wouldn't notice that Killer wasn't around. At the same time, he was planning to pay a visit to Killer's previous handler, Hunt Hunter. She lived in Sugarview, and we hoped she might be able to help us. We'd even wondered if she might be the dognapper.

"Maybe she snatched Killer because she missed him," Joe had proposed, looking hopeful.

That didn't seem too likely to me. Hunt had to know she'd be first on the suspect list. But I hadn't bothered to say so. Why bum Joe out?

The bell startled me out of my thoughts. Gathering up my books, I hurried to my next class.

I caught up to Lee in front of the door. "Hey, Frank," he greeted me. "How are you feeling?

Hope that fall yesterday didn't take too much out of you."

He sounded as friendly as ever. I wondered if he'd missed the news about that blog post. I'd noticed a few suspicious looks from others. Under the circumstances, it was the least of my concerns. But it was a constant reminder that time was running out for this mission.

"Still a little muscle sore. But I'll live," I told Lee. "Listen, I saw Destiny in the infirmary while I was there. She okay?"

Lee looked worried. "Yeah, she's finally getting better," he said. "But whatever she ate yesterday really hit her hard. She still couldn't keep much down this morning."

"Really?" I hoped I didn't sound as surprised as I felt. I'd assumed Destiny was faking. But if she was, it sounded as if she had Lee fooled.

And what if she *wasn't* faking? Darity was still one of our suspects; the only one with easy access to the medication we'd found in the Winner's Cup. But now I had to wonder. Would he really poison his own daughter—not just once, but twice? Despite our concerns about his honesty, I just wasn't convinced he'd do that. It was clear that he cared about Destiny, even if the two of them didn't have the best relationship.

But there was someone else on our suspect list who wouldn't hesitate to do that much and more. Nigel Nabb. Everyone said that if he couldn't find a good story, he wasn't above creating one. Could that be what he was doing right now?

"Frank?" Lee poked me in the arm. "Earth to Frank. You're a million miles away."

I snapped out of it, forcing a smile. "Sorry," I said, heading for my desk. "Just thinking about our quiz today."

At dinner that night, Lee shoveled one last bite of mystery meat into his mouth and stood up. "Catch you guys later," he said. "I've got some cramming to do for tomorrow's science test."

I couldn't help remembering that bus ticket we'd found in his room. Would Lee even *be* at Firth tomorrow to take that test?

But I didn't have time to worry about that. A few minutes later I spotted Joe tiptoeing toward the exit.

"I'd better bounce too," I said, grabbing my tray. "Later, guys."

"See you," said Spencer. Most of the others just grunted or waved and returned to their conversation. It had mostly revolved around Nigel Nabb. He'd been all over campus that day, filming and interviewing people. It sounded like he was digging for any dirt he could find. Including the real reason for Ellery's sudden departure. I had no idea where he'd heard about that one, but I hoped he wouldn't track it back to us. That was all we—or ATAC—needed.

I hurried to catch up with Joe. He was still sneaking along.

"Hey," I hissed into his ear. "Where's that dog of yours?"

He jumped about a foot in the air and spun around. When he saw it was only me, he scowled. "Real funny, bro."

I grinned. Sometimes it's impossible to resist messing with him.

But my smile faded fast. "Come on, let's get out of here before anyone asks after Killer for real."

"I'm with you." Joe shot a look at the headmasters' table. "At least Dr. Montgomery and that eagle-eyed old biddy sidekick of his aren't here tonight. They'd be sure to notice their precious canine tradition wasn't around."

Sure enough, the seats usually occupied by Montgomery and Mrs. Wilson were empty. That wasn't too unusual. The pair often took their meals at the Cottage.

"Don't freak out," I told Joe. "It's not like you

usually bring Killer to dinner with you anyway."

"Okay. Still, the sooner we get out of here, the better I'll feel."

I couldn't argue with him there. Soon we were safely outside at the edge of the Green. It was a chilly, breezy night. That meant nobody was strolling around outside to overhear us. Good.

"So how was your trip to Sugarview?" I asked Joe. "Anything to report?"

"Not really. Hunt wasn't home. Her brother said she's in Maine at some dog show or something."

Great. Another dead end.

"Okay, here's what I found out today. . . ." I quickly told him about Destiny's food poisoning.

"Are you sure Lee was telling the truth?" Joe asked. "Maybe he was covering for his girlfriend."

"Maybe. But it didn't seem like it." I shrugged. "Anyway, I'm really starting to lean toward Nigel as our top suspect."

"Really?" said Joe. "I mean, yeah, the guy is scum. But don't forget, he wasn't even on campus yet when most of the stuff went down."

"I know. But maybe we're getting too hung up on the timing here." I turned and started wandering down the walk with Joe beside me. "Trying too hard to force all the incidents into one pattern.

Which doesn't make much sense, seeing that we've already nabbed two separate culprits."

"I guess."

"So maybe we should just focus on the most serious and recent incidents and take it from there." I glanced at him. "And from that perspective, like I said, Nigel looks like our best bet."

Joe raised one eyebrow. "I can't believe this," he said. "Did we, like, switch personalities when I wasn't paying attention? Because usually *you're* the stickler for working out all the details, and *I'm* the one who's all freewheeling and ready to leave stuff out."

"So are you saying you're not on board?"

"Nope." He grinned. "Let's go with it. Now that you mention it, Nigel *is* a pretty tasty suspect. He has a lot of resources and stuff behind him. You know, what with the TV production studio and all . . ."

"Exactly." I nodded. "He could have started all the rumors that have been flying around here. He could even be the one behind the FirthFirst blog. His researchers might have been able to dig up that medical info and my true ID."

"We already suspected him of vandalizing Darity's house to create more of a story," Joe added. "And he did turn up the same day that bomb went off at GTT. I'm sure someone on his staff knows enough about basic chemistry to have pulled that one off, whether they got the ingredients here at Firth or brought them from somewhere else. Come to think of it, maybe that person in the hoodie I chased was someone working for Nigel."

"Right. And after that little incident at the pool . . ."

"Nigel probably has a grudge against Killer," Joe finished grimly. "Hello, dognapping. Not to mention he's probably not crazy about me and Destiny, either. Think he put something in her food?"

"Not sure how he'd manage that, but you never know. Maybe we can question her later about what she ate yesterday." I rotated my arm as we walked, trying to work out some lingering soreness from my fall.

Joe noticed. "So what about the rope thing? How could Nigel guess that Montgomery was going to make you guys climb it? Let alone that *you'd* be the one shimmying up there when it broke?"

"I'm thinking maybe that was just an accident." I shrugged. "Anyway, we're freewheeling it here, remember? Let's not get too caught up in the loose ends."

"So what do we do now? Confront him with the evidence and see what he says?"

"Yeah. It's getting late, but we should track him down first thing tomorrow."

"Why wait?" Joe pointed across the darkening Green. "There he is now."

He was right. Nigel himself was hurrying along the path on the far side of the lawn. Even at this distance, I could see the little red "record" light on his camcorder blinking away.

"Quick, don't let him out of sight!" I took off across the grass with Joe right behind me.

When we caught up to Nigel, he was talking to himself. Or rather, to his camera. Some kind of voiceover stuff, maybe.

"Mr. Nabb," I called as we neared him. "We need to talk to you about something."

He glanced over at us. When he recognized Joe, he frowned.

"Oh. It's dog boy," he said. "Sorry, lads. I'm busy."

"It's important," Joe insisted. "Come with us, okay? There's a place nearby where we can talk in private."

"Sorry, lads." Nigel kept hurrying along in the direction he'd been going. "No time for chitchat. Just got a hot tip on some barmy upper-crust secret-society ritual going down any second now. It's going to be gold—I don't want to miss a thing."

Joe and I traded a look. Secret-society ritual? Was he talking about the Brothers of Erebus? Could the shadowy group still have something to do with all this?

"Let's let him go, then tag along and see what's up," Joe whispered, holding me back as Nigel rushed on. "We can always bust him afterward."

"Sounds like a plan."

We let Nigel get a head start, then started tailing him. He was rushing along toward the woods at the edge of the manicured campus, not seeming to notice we were following.

"Think he's heading for that old hunting cabin in the woods where all that other BoE stuff went down?" I whispered.

Joe shrugged. "Kinda looks that way. If he turns down that path, we'll know he—hey, what's he doing?"

Nigel had stopped just short of the forest's edge. One of the Firth golf carts was parked there. The school maintained a small fleet of the carts, which were outfitted in the Firth colors. I'd seen them shuttling elderly guests around campus and being used for other errands.

"Brilliant!" Nigel's loud, distinctive voice drifted back to us on the cool breeze. Talking to himself again. "Now I won't have to ruin my Ferragamos slogging through the mud and snow in this god-forsaken place. . . ."

"Quick," Joe hissed. "He's going to commandeer that cart! We'll never be able to keep up on foot."

I was already darting forward. Nigel had been pretty quick to tell us where he was going, which meant he wasn't too concerned about keeping it secret. Maybe if we asked nicely, he'd let us ride along with him. Especially if we promised to share lots of juicy Firth gossip on the way.

Joe was clearly thinking along the same lines. "You do the talking, bro," he said, putting on a burst of speed as Nigel climbed into the vehicle and reached for the ignition. "He's more likely to—"

BLAM!

I was knocked flat on my back as the golf cart exploded in a fiery blast.

Out of Time

I hit the ground hard. Beside me, I heard Frank let out a surprised "Oof!"

A quick glance showed him looking dazed but okay. I pushed myself to my feet. All my parts still seemed to be in working order. Good.

I glanced ahead at the remains of the golf cart. Not so good.

"Nigel?" I called, racing forward.

It was still hot up there from the explosion. I could feel it on my feet, even through the soles of my shoes. Flames licked at the twisted metal and plastic chunks.

When I got a little closer, my stomach started to churn. I turned away and hurried back to Frank, who had just climbed to his feet with a groan.

"Nigel?" he asked.

"Dead." I shuddered. "*Way* dead."

Frank looked grim. He glanced over his shoulder as several shouts came from the direction of the cafeteria.

"Guess everyone heard the blast," he said. "What should we do?"

"Blend in, I guess." I bit my lip, shooting a quick glance in the direction of our top suspect. What was left of him, anyway. "Because I'm thinking we may still be here for a while."

Frank shook his head. "Just when we thought we had this mission nailed down . . ."

There was no more time for conversation. The shouts and confused voices were getting closer. Frank and I split up and melted into the gathering crowd.

I found myself surrounded by chattering freshmen. They were all excited about yet another explosion on campus. Guess they hadn't expected prep school to be so much like an action movie.

Glancing around, I spotted Dr. Montgomery. He was hobbling over from the direction of his home.

Seeing him reminded me of something. He was a Brother of Erebus. His name had been on the list Frank had seen on Darity's computer. Plus, Montgomery had all but admitted it before. And Nigel had been rushing off in search of the secret society. Maybe this was a good time to ask the former headmaster a few questions about the mysterious group.

"Hello, sir," I said, falling into step with him.

Montgomery peered ahead. People were milling around the site of the explosion. There were a few shrieks. Probably people getting a look at the body.

I felt a flash of guilt. Frank and I were better equipped to handle that kind of sight than the average high school kid. Should we have stayed put and chased people off until the cops—or at least Dr. Darity—arrived on the scene?

I pushed the thought aside. We'd gotten away with doing that once before when Lewis was killed. But our cover was a lot shakier now. If we played traffic cops again, especially after the implications on the blog, there was no way we'd be able to stick around at Firth any longer.

"What's going on, my boy?" Montgomery asked me, leaning heavily on his cane for support.

"I'm not exactly sure." That much was the truth, anyway. "I think it was that reporter, Nigel Nabb."

Montgomery shot me a sharp-eyed look. "You can be straight with me," he said quietly. "I know you're ATAC, remember?"

That's right. I'd almost forgotten.

"Okay," I said. "It *was* Nabb. We were tailing him—he said he was going to film some secret-society ritual going on tonight. I'm guessing it was the Brothers of Erebus."

"What?" Montgomery pursed his lips and shook his head. "That's ridiculous. There's no ritual happening tonight, or I'd know about it." Then he caught himself. "Er, if there were such a group as the Brothers of Erebus anymore, of course . . ."

I was about to remind him that *he* could be straight with *me*. After all, I'd been there to hear Ellery's confession.

Instead I decided to let it drop. I'd just noticed that Spencer was among the students milling around. He was a BoE member, so if there was a ritual, he'd surely be out there in the woods instead of here. So maybe Montgomery was right and there was no ritual. Had somebody lied to Nigel to lure him to his doom?

Another thought occurred to me. We didn't know how Nigel had heard about the ritual. What if the lie had actually been meant for Frank and me? What if we were the ones who were supposed to be tempted by that golf cart parked oh-so-conveniently at the head of the trail?

The thought made me queasy. But I pushed it aside, doing my best to focus on the facts.

I looked around. Patton was goggling at the scene nearby. So were most of the GTT guys. Destiny was standing alone, staring at the wreckage. Her boyfriend, Lee, was nowhere in sight. My heart sank. Did that mean something?

Dr. Montgomery was still standing there, watching the flames. His lined face was sad and tired.

"It's just too bad this had to happen," he muttered. "If Darity hadn't pushed things . . ."

"Sir?" I wasn't sure whether he was talking to me or himself. I guess it was the latter. Because he just looked at me and then turned away.

My hands clenched in frustration. Why did the former headmaster have to be so prim and proper all the time? I had a feeling he'd been about to say something critical. Something about Darity. Possibly something that could help us crack this case.

But I was pretty sure it wouldn't do any good to question him. He was too genteel to come out and criticize the current headmaster, no matter what. Firth First . . .

I heard a buzz and reached for my pocket. But it wasn't my phone. It was Montgomery's.

He pulled out a cell phone. No, not just a cell phone—a super-high-tech PDA. He glanced at it, then started texting back a response, his gnarled fingers flying over the tiny keys.

I couldn't help being surprised. Montgomery was an old-fashioned guy—it was like seeing Shakespeare typing up *Macbeth* on a laptop while listening to his iPod. Okay, maybe not that bad. But I never would have pegged the old guy as a techie.

"Joe!" Dr. Darity hurried toward me, looking pale and anxious. "There you are. Where's Killer? The authorities are on their way, but I was thinking Killer might be able to pick up some clues before they arrive."

Uh-oh. "Um, Killer's not here," I said.

Darity looked impatient. "Could you go get him, please? Your cottage isn't far, and I really think we—"

"No, that's the thing." I swallowed hard. "Killer's, um, missing."

"Missing?"

"Dognapped."

Darity stared at me as if I'd just started speaking a different language. But he recovered quickly. "Are you sure?" he hissed, lowering his voice. "My God, whatever you do, don't let Dr. Montgomery know!" He looked nervously toward the former headmaster, who was still bent over his PDA nearby. "If he thinks he's lost one more beloved Firth tradition, it'll probably kill him!"

"Don't worry," I whispered back. "We're keeping

it on the DL until we figure out what's going on."

I stopped as Mrs. Wilson suddenly appeared on the scene. She started to hurry toward Dr. Montgomery. Then she spotted me and stopped short.

"What's *he* still doing here?" she demanded in a loud voice, jabbing a finger in my direction.

Darity blinked, looking taken aback. "Er, what do you mean?"

The housekeeper glared at me. "Everyone knows that dog disappeared yesterday and hasn't been seen since," she declared loudly. By now, several people were staring at us curiously. "Didn't you fire the last girl for much less?"

I froze in horror. But my mind was still clicking along. Was the glare she was giving me extra suspicious? I flashed back to the day Frank and I had paid a visit to the Cottage to talk to Montgomery. That was when we'd first discovered that he knew our true ID. While we were leaving, Mrs. Wilson had appeared. We hadn't been sure if she'd overheard the conversation or not.

I still wasn't sure. She was never exactly pleasant even at the best of times. And if she felt as strongly about school tradition as her boss, it was no wonder she'd react this way if she thought Killer was missing.

"Um, Killer's just been under the weather," I

stammered out, too startled to come up with a better excuse. "He—he's staying at the vet's office in town for a day or two."

I scurried off before she could say any more. Luckily, there was so much chaos it was easy to disappear into the crowd, smoke, and darkness.

Frank was watching the school security guards hold the crowd back. A couple of the guards looked a little queasy. I guessed they didn't see too many casualties of this type on the sleepy little campus.

Pulling Frank aside, I filled him in. "Oh, man," he said, rubbing his forehead. "Our cover is breaking up faster than ever. How'd Mrs. Wilson find out about Killer?"

"Who knows? Everyone says she sees all and knows all around this place." I shrugged. "Anyway, we've got to work fast."

"No kidding." Frank looked grim. "I'd say we have maybe twelve hours max to solve this. Otherwise we're going to have to pull out and let someone else handle it."

I wanted to argue. We'd never quit on a mission before, and I hated to think we might have to do it now. But I knew he was right. Still, twelve hours was twelve hours.

"Okay," I said. "So what's our next move?"

• • •

The dorm hallway was dim and quiet. Everyone was still out at the blast scene. *Almost* everyone.

Frank and I had sneaked off just far enough to discuss our suspect list. It was getting smaller all the time. Nigel was off, obviously. And so was Darity. We'd realized that he couldn't have rigged that golf cart. It hadn't been there when I'd passed by on my way to dinner, or I would have seen it. And Darity had already been in the caf when I'd arrived.

We'd discussed the possibility that he could have an accomplice. But neither of us was feeling him as a suspect anymore. Among other reasons, I'd noted how surprised he'd seemed when I'd told him about Killer being missing. The guy just didn't seem like that good an actor.

That left only one likely suspect on the list. Lee.

Who else could it be? Once we got past his Mr. Nice Guy demeanor and the inspiring life story, it actually made a lot of sense. He was probably the only one on our list who could have pulled off everything.

He was a star of the soccer team, which meant nobody would look twice at him going in or out of the coach's office. Like to smear that grease on the floor that had caused the swim coach's tumble.

Lee worked in the school office. That gave him

access to the computer records, which would have made it easy for him to change his own grades. Although why he would do that was still not clear.

He could have planted that bomb at the GTT house as easily as anyone, especially since we hadn't seen him around that day. And he might have tainted the Winner's Cup to throw suspicion off himself. Stealing that key could have given him access to Darity's house for the vandalism.

And now this. When we'd started looking around for him in the crowd at the bomb site, he wasn't there. And Frank remembered that he'd left dinner a little early.

And of course, there was that ticket back to Boston, almost as if he'd been planning to run away tonight after one last spectacular stunt. . . .

"He might already be gone," I murmured as we tiptoed toward his room. "That bus leaves in, like, three hours. He might have wanted to make sure he was early so he didn't miss it."

Frank shook his head. "I'm guessing he'll stick around long enough to see the results of his latest stunt. Criminals always seem to do that."

I was quiet for a moment as we crept along the deserted hallway. "Why do you think he did it?" I said at last. "Think all the teasing about being a charity case finally drove him over the edge?"

"We can figure out the psychological details later," Frank whispered. "If we want to wrap this up, let's try to stay focused."

I shrugged. We were almost at Lee's door anyway.

We stopped in front of it, listening.

"Just go ahead and knock," I whispered. "We're on the third floor—it's not like he can go out the window or anything."

Frank nodded. Taking a deep breath, he rapped sharply on the door. "Lee?" he called. "It's Frank. I need to talk to you."

There was no answer.

For some reason, my mind jumped to Killer. He was the one piece of the puzzle we hadn't really discussed.

"Think Killer could be in there?" I whispered with a flash of hope.

"Let's find out." Frank let out a whistle. "Killer? Here, boy!" he called.

Silence. My heart sank. So much for that—if his beloved Frank called him, Killer would definitely find a way to respond.

"This is ridiculous," I hissed. Let's just break down the door already. Or at least call Darity to let us in."

"I have a better idea." Frank backed away from

the door. "Let's stake out the dorm and see if he comes out."

"What? Why?"

"We don't really have any solid evidence against Lee right now. And like I said, a lot of criminals can't resist sticking around and visiting the scene of their crime. Maybe Lee will sneak out to see his handiwork before he takes off for town—and give us some more solid proof that he's our guy."

Okay, I had to admit that made sense. "He might go visit Destiny to say good-bye too," I said. "If Lee *does* have Killer, maybe he will stop off to release him from wherever he's got him hidden." I swallowed back the rest of what I was thinking: *If Killer is still alive.*

"Yeah. That would definitely give us enough proof to bust him." Frank turned down the hall. "Let's find a spot outside."

We set up our stakeout in some bushes with a good view of the dorm's main entrance. The back door was always locked after nine p.m. If Lee left the building, we'd see him.

Soon after we got settled, people started drifting back in from the explosion scene. We could hear some of the chatter as they passed us. Most people didn't seem too sure what had happened. Or even that there had been someone killed in the blast.

It was kind of fun to sit there and listen to everyone go by. No matter how long I'm in ATAC, playing spies never gets old.

But eventually things quieted down. After that, nothing happened for a while. A *long* while.

I started to yawn. It had been a busy day. My eyes started drooping. I had to pinch myself every few minutes to stay awake.

Soon my arms were black and blue from all the pinching. Well, not really. But I did realize I actually missed having Killer around. If he'd been here, he'd be keeping watch with no chance of sleepiness.

The campus grew darker. And quieter. Lights flicked off in the dorms. Stereos went silent. I could almost feel people falling asleep all around us.

Then, finally, something happened. Namely, Frank poked me in the arm.

"There he is!" he hissed.

I realized I'd been dropping off again. But I came awake instantly. Peering out of the bushes, I saw Lee's tall, skinny figure hurrying past us. His hands were in his pockets and his head was down.

"Come on," I mouthed.

We crawled out and followed him. He didn't head for Destiny's house as I'd expected. Instead he went straight into the woods, following a familiar path. He pulled out a flashlight as soon as he left the glow of the campus lanterns, clicking it on to light his way.

Once again I found myself missing Killer. He was surefooted and silent moving through the dark forest.

Me and Frank, not so much. Especially since we didn't have lights. Who knew we'd end up in a late-night hike through the woods?

We barely managed to keep up with Lee without giving ourselves away. The only thing that kept us on track was Lee's flashlight. I kept my eyes on its bobbing beam and did my best not to trip over the roots and stones that kept jumping into our path.

Finally the beam stopped. Lee had reached that hunting cabin in the woods. Was that where Killer was stashed? Was Lee meeting Destiny here for one last romantic encounter? Or was he getting ready to set another trap on his way out of town?

Lee disappeared into the cabin. Frank and I crept forward. Then we heard the sound of voices.

"Shh," Frank hissed, dropping down behind some brush. "He's not alone."

I strained my ears. The second voice was kind of high-pitched. Destiny? I wasn't quite sure.

"We've got the element of surprise," I breathed into Frank's ear. "Let's just take them down."

Frank hesitated, then nodded. "Wait till they come out into the clearing," he murmured in my ear. "I'll take whoever's on the right, you go left."

"Got it."

We didn't have long to wait. Lee and the other figure emerged after just a minute or two. Both of them had flashlights, which they were shining straight ahead of them. Directly into our eyes. That made it impossible to see who was behind the lights.

But it didn't matter. Whoever it was, it was time to end this. The figures moved toward the path to campus.

"Three, two . . . ," Frank whispered.

One.

We both leaped forward. I heard a cry of surprise from Frank's target. It was Lee.

Meanwhile I tackled the other person. "Gotcha!" I cried, taking him or her down. It wasn't hard; whoever it was was small. Really small.

The figure struggled, but I was able to pin him or her down easily. I grabbed the flashlight out of the person's hand.

"Let's see who we have here," I said, turning the light on my victim's face. When I saw what face was staring back at me, I did a double take. "Huh?" I blurted out.

Secrets Revealed

"Who are you?" I heard Joe ask in amazement. Glancing over, I saw that he had a kid pinned down. "Take it easy on him, okay?" Lee said from beneath me. "He's only twelve."

I loosened my grip. "Maybe you'd better tell us what this is about."

So he did. It turned out the second figure was Tommy Lewicki's little brother. He'd run away from his—and Lee's—old Boston neighborhood after getting in trouble with the cops for shoplifting.

"I didn't want to steal that stuff," the kid spoke up at that point, sounding on the verge of tears. "They made me."

"It's okay, Mikey," Lee told him. Then he

turned to face Joe and me. "Neighborhood bullies," he said with a grimace. "The same gang that's been making trouble since I was Mikey's age." He shrugged. "Had some problems with them myself back then. But I owned up to it, and look at me now."

He went on to explain that he'd finally convinced both Tommy and his brother that Mikey should go back to Boston and do the same thing. Own up to his petty crime. Try to make things right—just like Lee. Based on the way the kid was looking at him, it was clear that Lee was his hero.

"So that's who the bus ticket is for," I mused.

Lee shot me a look. "You knew about that?" he said. "How?"

Joe and I traded a glance. "It's a long story," Joe said. "So you had Mikey stashed away out here all week?"

"Well, here and my dorm room, and sometimes Tommy's. We've just been trying to keep him out of sight."

That explained all the junk food wrappers under Lee's bed.

Anyway, I told Tommy I'd get Mikey to the bus," Lee went on. "Figured I had a better chance of pulling it off. Tommy's great, but he can be kind of jumpy." He smiled as Mikey giggled. "Plus, I figured if we did get caught, I had a better shot at talking my way through it. Dr. Darity likes me."

I was surprised that Lee was so aware of being the headmaster's pet. But maybe I shouldn't have been. The guy was pretty sharp. Otherwise he wouldn't be here.

"Okay," I said. "But why'd you steal that key out of Darity's office?"

Once again, Lee looked startled. "How'd you—?" he began. Then he shook his head. "It was the master key that opens a bunch of campus buildings. Including the kitchen in the caf."

"To get food for Mikey." Joe nodded.

I could tell he was convinced that Lee was telling the truth. So was I. The things he was telling us explained pretty much all his mysterious behavior lately. And of course there was Exhibit A sitting right in front of us. Mikey.

That reminded me. "You'd better hit the road if you want to make that bus," I said, checking my watch. "It leaves in, like, forty minutes."

Lee jumped to his feet, looking alarmed. "Oh, man. Is it really that late? We'll never make it in time!"

"What do you mean? Sugarview's only a twenty-minute drive," said Joe.

"Yeah—in a car." Lee shook his head, looking defeated. "All we've got are bikes."

"Do you have a license?" I asked. When Lee nodded, I fished out my key ring and detached the key to our rental car. "Here you go—take our wheels."

"Are you serious?" Lee looked relieved. "Thanks, guys. Come on, squirt, let's get moving." As Mikey hurried out of the clearing, Lee paused and looked back. "Hey—thanks for being cool about this. And I hope maybe sometime you'll tell me who you guys *really* are, okay?"

Joe and I just smiled and waved. Lee waved back and hurried off.

Then Joe turned to face me. "Now what?"

"I don't know." I sighed and sank back down onto the log. "It looks like we've eliminated all our likely suspects."

"Except Nigel. Someone else eliminated him for us."

I stood up. "Let's head back to campus. We can talk about it on the way."

"What's this?"

I stopped in mid-yawn. We'd just reached Joe's cottage. He was staring at something pinned to the door. A note.

"What's it say?" I asked, instantly on alert.

Joe ripped the note off the door and read it aloud.

"'Come to Firth Hall immediately if you ever want to see Killer alive again.'" He gasped. "Oh, man! How long do you think this has been here?"

I didn't have an answer for that. It was after midnight by now. And Joe hadn't been here since leaving for dinner hours earlier.

"So do we go?" I asked. "It could be a trap."

"Oh, it's so *totally* a trap!" Joe exclaimed. "But we've got to go. What choice do we have?"

"I guess you're right. We've got no suspects. No new clues. And whoever wrote this has Killer." I shrugged. "Plus, there are two of us, and we're trained in this. We'll just have to be careful and hope for the best."

Firth Hall was pretty spooky even during broad daylight. In the middle of the night? Majorly creepy.

We pushed through the front door, which wasn't locked. The main foyer was dark and echoey. Creaks and other old-building-type sounds came from all directions, muffled by the thick walls and sheer size of the place. There were crazy shadows everywhere; the only light came from moonlight pouring in through the milky glass of the ancient windows.

There were some light switches on the wall

near the door. I threw a couple of them on. Nothing happened. Surprise, surprise. Luckily, we'd grabbed our flashlights from the cottage. I switched mine on. Its strong but thin beam barely seemed to pierce the dusty air around us.

"Now what?" Joe whispered, turning on his flashlight as well.

I didn't have to answer. Just then we both heard the faint sound of a bark.

"Killer!" Joe hissed. "Wait. Or is it?"

"What other dog is likely to be barking in here?" I shot him a look.

He rolled his eyes. "Okay, okay. Come on, let's find him."

I spun in a circle, feeling disoriented. The darkness and the constant settling noises of the old building could play tricks with you. "Maybe this way?"

I pointed down the hall. At that moment there was another bark. Still faint and faraway.

"Definitely that way," said Joe, charging off in that direction.

So much for being careful . . .

We followed the sound down that hallway and up a set of stairs. The barks came at irregular intervals, sometimes sounding louder, sometimes softer.

"Someone must be leading him around," Joe whispered as we paused on the third-floor landing to listen. "Just luring us here and there."

"Okay, but why?" The longer this went on, the less I was liking it. "What do they want from us?"

Joe didn't have an answer for that. So he did what he always does when he's not sure about something. Plunged onward, full speed ahead. When the next bark came, he raced off after it.

"This way!" he called over his shoulder.

We made our way up and down and around Firth Hall's dark, echoing corridors. Eventually the barks led us through the main floor and down another set of steps into the basement.

If we'd thought the rest of Firth Hall was the creepiest place on campus, now we knew better. The basement was a warren of cobwebby rooms and narrow, twisting hallways interspersed with echoing, cavernous spaces. There was no light at all down there except what leaked in through the slitlike windows located at ceiling level here and there. As in the rest of the building, the overheads were dead. Good thing we had those flashlights.

Finally the barking started to get louder. "I think we're catching up," Joe panted as we clambered over a loose stack of cinder blocks in a narrow hallway.

I just nodded. As best I could tell, we had to be near the back of the building by now. It was clear this section of the basement didn't get much use. Dusty cobwebs hit us in the face at almost every step, and the door handles were rusty and squealed when we turned them.

WOOF!

Joe spun around, shining his flashlight down a side hall I hadn't even noticed. "I think that came from down there!" he cried. "Come on!"

"Be—," I began. But he'd already disappeared into the darkness ahead, his light barely a pinprick in the gloom. "Careful," I finished with a sigh, hurrying after him.

I caught up to him in a small room at the far end of the hallway. He was casting his light around in there.

"Killer?" he called, taking a step farther in. He glanced back when he heard me enter. "You call him. He likes you better."

"Killer?" I whistled softly. "Here, boy."

There was no answer. Joe was still shining his light around. "Hey," he said as the beam picked up something small and dark in the corner. "What's that?"

I shone my own light that way. "Looks like an old-fashioned tape deck," I said. "But what—"

My voice trailed off in a gasp as there was another loud bark—coming right from that tape recorder!

"It's a trap!" Joe cried. "We have to—"

SLAM!

Before we could turn around, the thick metal door behind us crashed shut. I flung myself at it, but it was no use.

"It's locked!" I cried. I pounded on it. "Hey! Whoever you are, let us out of here!"

Joe didn't say anything. When I glanced back, he had a strange expression on his face.

"Do you smell something?" he asked.

I stopped and sniffed the air. A distinctive odor met my nostrils. Metallic and vaguely fruity. It tickled the back of my throat, making me cough.

"Is that . . ."

"Chlorine gas," Joe finished grimly. He pointed to a metal grate covering an air vent in the floor. A deadly pale green cloud was pouring up out of it, rapidly filling the room.

I tugged the neck of my shirt up to cover my nose and mouth. "We've got to find a way out. Fast!"

ur Sure

'd always taken breathing for granted. Not anymore. Every breath I took, I felt more of the toxic gas trickling into my lungs. Nearby, I heard Frank wheezing as he struggled against the thickening cloud.

We'd already tried to get at the canister of gas. But it was locked safely beneath that metal grate. Without tools, there was no way to pry it open.

There was no way to get the door open either. We'd tried crashing our way through and ended up with nothing but bruised shoulders. The door was solid.

"The window," I choked out, pointing upward. "It's our only chance."

Frank peered up, his eyes watering. "Too . . . high . . . ," he gasped.

I wanted to argue. But I knew he was right. The window was up near the ceiling. Way too high to reach, even if we stood on each other's shoulders.

I sank to the floor, wheezing. It just wasn't worth fighting it anymore. Maybe it was better just to give up . . . to go to sleep . . .

CRASH!

My eyes flew open at the sound of shattering glass. A furry shape flew down through the muggy air.

"K-Killer?" I gasped out in amazement.

This had to be a dream. But no—a second later I felt a moist, cool nose nudging me. Killer barked loudly. Right in my ear.

"Ow," I mumbled as he trotted away.

But my mind was already clearing a little. So was the gas. It was escaping through the broken window overhead.

"Killer?" a woman's voice called, sounding confused. There was a cough. "Hey, who's down there?"

I heard Frank mumble something to Killer. A second later the dog returned to me. He nudged me again.

Slurp.

A wet tongue slapped against my face. I couldn't help smiling.

"Thanks, boy," I said, giving the dog a pat. Aw, what the heck. I gave him a hug, okay? And for once, he seemed to tolerate it. Maybe even like it. At least a little.

I clambered to my feet and looked up. Hunt Hunter was peering in through the window. "What's going on down there?" she called.

"You!" I accused. "You were the one who took Killer! Why'd you try to kill us?"

"Kill you?" She sounded more confused than ever.

"Dude, it wasn't her." Frank had recovered quickly once the gas had dissipated. He was examining the tape recorder. "Check it out."

I gasped when I saw the notation etched neatly on the back panel. *Property of Myrna Wilson.*

"Mrs. Wilson?" I exclaimed. "But it can't be her. For one thing, she wouldn't be stupid enough to leave that here with her name on it."

"She didn't think there'd be anyone left alive in this room to see it." Frank looked grim. "Come on, let's get out of here. We need to catch her before she realizes she didn't kill us."

A few minutes later we were out. We'd explained the gist to Hunt, who had disappeared just long enough to find some rope to pull us out. The cold night air tasted clean and fresh.

Hunt was still kind of confused. But she tagged along—with Killer—as we raced over to Mrs. Wilson's little cottage behind the Cottage.

When she answered the door, she had a long bathrobe pulled tightly around her. "Do you know what time it is?" she snapped as she swung the door open.

Okay. If that was how she wanted to play it . . .

"Sorry," Frank said, not sounding sorry at all. "But we thought you'd want this back right away." He pulled the tape recorder out from behind his back.

Her face crumpled. She tried to hold it together, but it was obvious. She knew the jig was up.

"All right, you caught me." She tipped her head back proudly. "It was all me. I'll go quietly."

She grabbed her purse and marched toward the door. Frank and I traded a look. Whatever reaction we'd been expecting, this wasn't it.

"Um, okay," I said, hurrying after her.

At least I tried to. Killer had pushed his way in, and I had to stop to keep from tripping over his leash.

"Out of the way, fuzzy," I said, dodging around him.

At least I tried to. Killer moved forward, blocking my way. Not on purpose or anything. His nose was pressed to the floor, sniffing urgently.

"Come on, boy," I said, feeling my usual aggravation with the beast return. "This is no time to be nosing around for Scooby snacks."

"He's not looking for food." Hunt was watching the dog alertly. "There's someone else here."

"No there's not," Mrs. Wilson snapped. "Come along, I already told you it's me you want. It was all me!"

There was an edge of hysteria in her voice. Interesting. "Go find 'em, Killer," I said, keeping an eye on Mrs. Wilson.

"No!" she shrieked, diving at the dog. "Get out of here!"

Killer ignored her. He'd finally found his trail. Leaping ahead, he pulled Hunt farther into the house. Frank and I followed.

We burst into a room at the back. There we found a cowering figure.

"Dr. Montgomery?" Frank exclaimed.

"It's not my fault," he snapped, looking more like a cornered animal than the dapper elderly gentleman we knew. "I wasn't doing it for me. I was doing it for Firth! All for Firth!"

"Firth First!" Mrs. Wilson cried from behind us.

"Yes." Dr. Montgomery closed his eyes. "Firth First, Firth Always, Firth Forever."

"Ew." I made a face as I picked at a particularly gross chunk of bird crud. "I almost wish I was back at Firth picking up doggie doo."

Frank looked at me from the other side of the cage bars. We were back home in Bayport. It was a crisp late autumn afternoon. And what were we doing? That's right. Cleaning Playback's cage. Aunt Trudy never gives up.

At least it gave us a chance to talk over the mission in private. We'd barely had a moment alone since getting back.

"I still can't believe it was Dr. Montgomery all along," Frank mused. "We should have guessed sooner."

"How could we? Who suspects a doddering old man of that kind of stuff?" I flicked another plop of poo off the bars.

"True," Frank agreed, dipping his scrub brush in soapy water. "He never could have done most of it without Mrs. Wilson."

"Loyal to the end." I grimaced as I remembered the way she'd cursed at the police as they'd cuffed Montgomery.

But before that, he'd admitted to everything. It

turned out he didn't like the changes Dr. Darity was making at his beloved school all along. But what had sent him over the edge at the beginning of the semester was when Darity had accepted Lee, Tommy, and the other scholarship students, and then asked for Destiny to be admitted as well.

"From the way he was talking, it sounds like he went even nuttier when Lee and Destiny started doing so well," I said. "Destiny at soccer, and Lee in general."

Frank nodded. "Even being admitted to GTT and then the BoE."

That was when Montgomery had decided to try to scare those two away from Firth. And/or make Darity look bad. So he'd enlisted the help of his faithful—and equally snobby and tradition-bound—servant, Mrs. Wilson.

They'd done much of the early sabotage, including all the computer threats. It turned out Montgomery himself had taken care of the high-tech stuff. As a science teacher, being old-fashioned had its limits. He was actually quite the techie, as I'd noted after spotting his PDA.

Angry about Destiny and Lee making the varsity soccer team, he'd had Mrs. Wilson grease the soccer coach's floor to send a message. Unfortunately, the swim coach had been caught in the crossfire.

"I guess we should have paid attention when people told us Montgomery knew everything that went on at Firth," Frank said as he scrubbed at a perch. "Maybe we would've realized he'd be one of the few who knew about Destiny's blood supply."

"And that hunting cabin, and the old tunnels beneath campus," I added.

Montgomery had sent Mrs. Wilson to rig that runaway soccer truck. He'd had her tamper with Destiny's water bottle to give her food poisoning. He'd also set the bomb at the frat house and stolen the anticonvulsant drug by using his old master key.

"But what definitely should have tipped us off was the vandalism at the headmaster's house." Frank shook his head. "Only Mrs. Wilson would care about leaving all the Firth stuff intact and only trashing Darity's own stuff."

"Yeah. Then there was that rope trick." I shuddered as I remembered how close Frank had come to being badly hurt—or worse. "Montgomery must have had her rig that rope to break when someone was halfway up. And then he made sure it would be either you, Lee, or Destiny who fell."

"Guess he threw me in there because he thought we might be onto him." Frank shook his head. "If only he knew we had no idea!"

I nodded slowly, feeling kind of stupid. We'd missed so many clues. . . .

"Guess he started that FirthFirst blog to stir up resentment against the people he didn't like, including Darity," I said. "But it backfired when it caught Nigel Nabb's attention. I wonder why Montgomery waited so long to take Nigel out, anyway? It's not like he couldn't have had him kicked off as soon as he turned up on campus. He didn't have to kill him."

"I've been thinking about that." Frank stopped cleaning for a second and glanced at me. "My guess is at first he was tolerating Nigel hanging around because it was making Darity look bad. But when Montgomery realized just how sleazy Nigel and his show really were, he knew he couldn't let him drag his beloved Firth's name through the mud."

"Yeah, that makes sense. Though Mrs. Wilson claimed he only told her they couldn't let Nigel degrade Firth on national TV, and she did the rest."

We were both still pretty skeptical about that one. Mrs. Wilson had insisted to the police that she'd concocted the second explosion on her own, telling Montgomery she was only planning to blow up his equipment.

"Sounds like they're both sticking to that story," said Frank. "Maybe it's true."

"Or maybe it's just a faithful servant being loyal to the end." I shrugged. "Guess we'll never know. But either way, they'll both be in prison for a good long time. I'm just glad Hunt didn't end up there too. She comes across as kind of a loner or whatever. But she's okay."

Frank grinned. "You have to say that. She saved our lives."

"Yeah. She and Killer." I smiled fondly at the thought of the dog.

That's right, I said fondly. Now that I wasn't stuck walking the creature umpteen times a day, I actually missed Killer. A little. Okay, not really. But I'd never forget him, that's for sure.

"It's cool that Darity gave Hunt her old job back," Frank said. "I bet Killer's happy about that too."

I nodded. Hunt had confessed to the dognapping. Dr. Montgomery had approached her, promising that if she helped spirit Killer away from Firth, he'd pay both their ways to Canada so they could start a new life there, with more than enough cash for Hunt to open the dog training center she'd always dreamed of.

At first she'd gone along with the plan. But in the end she'd felt guilty. She loved hanging with Killer again but knew it was wrong to make it happen that way. Plus, she didn't really want to move to Canada and leave Mr. Westerley behind.

See, that was the one bit of Firth gossip that we'd known about and Montgomery hadn't. Hunt was dating Firth's English teacher.

So she'd been sneaking Killer back onto campus when he'd picked up the scent of that chlorine gas. I guess something in his training told him it was trouble. And you know the rest.

Anyway, Darity had seemed impressed by Hunt's (eventual) honesty. Plus, I guess he still felt bad for firing her the first time for false reasons. So he'd offered her old job back, and she'd gladly accepted.

"It's weird," I said, grabbing a sponge and squeezing it out. "I haven't heard a peep in the news about any of this."

"Except that blurb on *R and F Report*." Frank grimaced. "Remember? Aunt Trudy was all upset because Nigel Nabb was supposedly killed in 'a tragic motor vehicle accident while on location in New England.'"

"Hey, it's true. A golf cart counts as a motor vehicle." I soaped up one of Playback's perches.

"Still, like, wow. Firth really knows how to cover up a juicy story!"

"Yeah." Frank glanced at me. "Like the truth about the Brothers of Erebus."

He had a point. We never had gotten to the bottom of the shadowy secret society. At least not this time. Maybe someday we'd track down the truth.

Maybe. Either way, this was one mission I was relieved to have closed at last. After our time at Firth, it was almost a relief to be back scrubbing bird poop under Aunt Trudy's watchful eye.

Almost.